D0497904

The
Tenor
Saxophonist's
Story

ALSO BY JOSEF ŠKVORECKÝ

THE Tenor Saxophonist's STORY

JOSEF ŠKVORECKÝ

Translated by
Caleb Crain,
Káča Poláčková Henley,
and Peter Kussi

THE ECCO PRESS

THE ECCO PRESS
100 West Broad Street
Hopewell, New Jersey 08525

Library of Congress Cataloging-in-Publication Data
Škvorecký, Josef.
    [Povídky tenorsaxofonisty. English]
    The tenor saxophonist's story / Josef Škvorecký ; translated by
  Caleb Crain, Káča Poláčková Henley, and Peter Kussi. — 1st ed.
      p.   cm.
    ISBN 0-88001-461-X
    I. Crain, Caleb. II. Poláčková-Henley, Káča. III. Kussi, Peter.
  IV. Title.
  PG5038.S527P6613   1997
  891.8'635—dc20   96-42534

Designed by Angela Foote
The text of this book is set in New Baskerville
9 8 7 6 5 4 3 2 1
FIRST EDITION

To Dan Halpern, who's always had trust in me.

Contents

The
Tenor
Saxophonist's
Story

Panta Rei

You can't step in the same river twice.

Heraclitus

In those days, I was only a baby fascist while my father was a big fascist, although he didn't think of himself like that. That's today's simplified way of putting it; in the old days these things were more complicated. I was a little bourgeois boy in velvet pants, with a polka-dot handkerchief tied under my chin, and I'd taunt Voženil: "Bolshevik, Bolshevik!" as I munched on my frankfurter. Voženil waited to see if I'd leave him a morsel, and when I didn't he called me "you pen-pushing greedygut" and I paid him back with "you Bolshevik." Each of us brought it from home: me with my velvet pants and suspenders decorated with airplanes and locomotives, Voženil with his big loud mouth that always gave off the sweet smell of bread (he never brushed his teeth), clodhoppers passed down from an older brother, dirty words which I never used because I knew from home that you weren't supposed to. Still, my father was a big, strong fascist, even though he didn't think of himself in that way. He marched in processions sporting a cane because he had a limp inherited from the First World War, and he wore a silver-gray shirt. I boasted about him to schoolmates and was very proud of him when I stood on the sidewalk with my mother, who held me by the hand, and we watched him striding down the street, we watched him scowl and sing and shout.

Once, however, I saw him weep, and I couldn't believe my own eyes. That was the time the Conservative leader Dr.

Kramář died. Dad's large, meaty mouth which ground away at dinnertime like a millstone now collapsed into a crooked curve resembling the tragic semicircle painted on the lips of the great comedian George Voskovec (described by Dad as a drawing-room Bolshevik and agent of Moscow), tears rolled down his smooth-shaven cheeks, tears as big as the pearls in Mother's necklace but glassy, transparent and damp. Dad sat in the cool, darkened drawing room, with its violet wallpaper, black piano and black furniture; only the gilded face of the grandfather clock glowed in the dusk. Tears as big as pearls, as big as drops of autumn rain kept dropping off Dad's vest. Facing him sat Mrs. Zkoumal, editor of *Národní Listy,* dressed in a black silk gown, her red hair upswept into a mikado. Her elegant hands, with red-enameled nails that extended a good centimeter beyond the fingertips, kept kneading a black-bordered handkerchief.

She moaned: "What a man! What a mind! A real giant! What a Czech! They don't come any finer! And they kept hounding him all his life! Bolsheviks, the Beneš crowd, clericals, the Castle, all of them! All of them are guilty! They hounded him to his grave! To deprive the nation of such a man! But they'll soon see what they have wrought!"

I didn't understand what was going on, while I sat in a chair in a black velvet suit, my feet dangling high above the floor, Mother next to me, also wearing black, not weeping

but looking sad. But then she always looked sad. I gazed in
fascination at that red-gold-rust-colored mikado hairdo of
Madam Editor, at her eyebrows as thin as a thread and
arched like Gothic vaults in the church, her slender legs in
silk stockings visible way past the knees because Madam
Editor had her legs crossed and though her gown was a
mourning gown it was also stylish, as could be expected
from a youthful star on the *Národní Listy* editorial staff.

That was the first time I saw—and heard—Madam Editor.

Then a couple of years quickly went by and a lot happened. The Germans sent Dad to a concentration camp,
because he took his nationalist convictions seriously. They
took away our apartment and Mother moved us to
Grandpa's house in the country.

One evening after the war, when I was already grown
up, and had exchanged my velvet shorts for stylish close-
cut trousers and played tenor sax in a jazz band, a man
came to see us one evening and handed Mother a crumpled letter which Dad had given him in Oranienburg.
Mother read it and started crying; she cried on and on—
from that day on she turned ever sadder and in the end
she stopped talking, only sat and stared. Then they took
her to an insane asylum.

That man told us how he and Dad slept in the same
bunk and helped each other as well as they could, though
they also argued. They argued on account of bolshevism.

Dad believed that the Czech nation would come to its senses after the war—meaning that the National Democratic party would take over the government—and he became furious when the man maintained that Comrade Stalin would see to it that things turned out differently. Dad was altogether naive. He even behaved insolently toward the SS troopers, and so in the end they did away with him.

After they took Mother to the asylum, Grandpa had a stroke and they kicked us out of the house. I moved to Prague, started to play tenor sax in Zetka's jazz band and became friends with Miss Julie Nedochodil, whose dad was a deputy of the Catholic Populist party. Not sensing anything wrong, he let me sublet a room in his beautiful modernist villa.

At his house I met Madam Editor for the second time.

She no longer wore a short gown, a red mikado hairdo nor long red claws on her fingers. She was dressed in a shapeless gray outfit, her feet were modestly ensconced in low-heeled shoes, her hair was set in nondescript waves and on her bosom—which was hard to make out under the guileless blouse—a gold cross. She was sitting in the dining room, where the conversation centered on materialism and spiritualism. She kept casting devout glances at Franciscan Father Urbanec and held forth:

"Such obvious nonsense," she said. "How can anybody believe such things? This world, this fascinating

universe filled with heavenly wonders, this body of
mine, all those amazing miracles of creation which
proclaim the glory of the Creator—can this be nothing but dead, uncreative, motionless matter?"

Father Urbanec kept nodding his head while his
hand nestled a cut-glass goblet in which a little puddle of
yellow wine from the Teplá cloister rolled gently from side
to side like a spoonful of honey. In the rays of the sun, fil-
tered through the greenery of Papa Nedochodil's lush garden, it emanated a golden glow into the dining room.
Father Urbanec was responsible for guiding converts and
Madam Editor was his sheep. She converted totally. She
switched from the banned *Národní Listy* to the still toler-
ated *Lidová Demokracie*. She took her son out of public high
school and enrolled him in the archbishop's school in Dejvice. She also launched a battle for the soul of her husband, and managed to return him to the pale of the
Church in the nick of time, as he lay on his deathbed. Before this long-suffering agnostic breathed his last, the rite
of a church wedding was performed with the assistance of
Father Urbanec, so that after fifteen years of civil cohabita-
tion their marriage became sanctified before God. The
place of Dr. Kramář in her heart was taken over by Father
Urbanec. She even chose him as her confessor, and on the
first Friday of every month pestered him with her sins,
which she committed mainly in thought, less frequently in
speech and hardly ever in action. She joined the Society of

Perpetual Veneration of the Consecrated Host, and also the Eucharistic Society of Saint Cypriana for reclaiming young women as novices. She also became a leader of Catholic Girl Scouts. She thus became—or rather, remained—a fighter against bolshevism, albeit under a new flag.

From that day on, I saw her quite often. She was a constant visitor at Papa Nedochodil's, picking his brains for political ideas. She took a critical stance toward me, because I favored wild neckties and striped socks and on Sundays, instead of going to church, I blew hot licks in a popular dance joint in Vinohrady and elsewhere. She also criticized the virtually Bolshevik opinions of Pavel Nedochodil, a boy whom his family considered something of a failure and who entered the Young Communist Movement. She feared for our souls; performed heroic apostolic labors left and right. She managed to bring Julie to the verge of tears when that attractive Catholic girl bought herself a two-piece swimsuit; she got Madam Nedochodil to cancel her subscription to *Kino;* and she exerted such strong influence over Papa Nedochodil that he stopped reading detective stories. She radiated sanctity and deep faith.

Then a miracle happened in Slovakia: two shepherd children in Malá Fatra had a vision of the Virgin Mary. Madam Editor took off at once in search of miracle and news story. She went in the company of journalists, consist-

ing of cynics from the communist *Rudé Právo* and sensa-
tion-seekers from *Svobodné Slovo*.

They came back a week later.

"You should have seen the cars, Doctor!" she reported
to a gathering that was headed by Papa Nedochodil and
Father Urbanec and that also included Julie with a somewhat uncatholically low-cut dress, and myself, sporting a
specially selected Bikini-Nagasaki necktie.

"Bumper-to-bumper traffic for miles! We had to get
out and walk, and only our newspaper passes got us
through the throngs. We reached the little hill where they
had put up a small, simple altar and at a quarter to three
they brought the two children. The Virgin was supposed to
appear at four, the hour of Christ's death. The children
knelt and prayed, and that whole throng of hundreds and
thousands knelt and prayed with them. Oh, Doctor! I've
never experienced such a blissful feeling in my life! And
then at four the children started to talk and we heard them
asking questions and answering—we didn't see nor hear
the Virgin but felt that she was there with us! And then a
priest took the children away and as for myself—I can tell
you, Doctor, I feel that I was present at a miracle!"

There was talk of visions and miracles, of Fatima, La
Salette, Bernadette, stigmata, the holy shroud of Turin,
and in the end, as usual, the conversation passed to the
subject of communism and communists. Madam Editor recounted her experiences in this regard:

"It's a moral morass, Doctor! Those people lack the most basic moral sense! I am ashamed to talk about it, I really feel myself blushing—but I have to tell you what sort of people they are! Just imagine, Doctor! We spent the night in Bratislava in the Winston Hotel and the editors from *Rudé Právo*—well, you can imagine how they joked about the miracle! They blasphemed in a way I wouldn't dare to repeat. Right after dinner I went to my room—and . . . I really don't know if I can say it with Julie sitting right here . . . "

She nodded her head in the direction of the half-bared bosom of my companion, who responded with a grimace.

"But I'll say it straight out, so that all of you get the picture of that crowd. Just imagine, one of the *Rudé Právo* editors—a widower with two children—followed me and grabbed me upstairs in the hall—of course, he smelled like a brewery—and he wanted—no, I'm too ashamed— he wanted me—well, he wanted me to do his bidding! Doctor! Forgive me for saying it, under normal conditions such a thing would never pass my lips, I just want you to know with what sort of element we have the honor of dealing. And he made me a marriage proposal! But first he wanted . . . well, Doctor, that's bolshevism for you! In the afternoon, they witness an unforgettable moment on Malá Fatra and just a few hours later they're back in the gutter . . . "

Then came February.

Disaster.

They threw Papa Nedochodil out of Parliament and Madam Editor off the paper.

They gave her a job in a factory.

I was thrown off the faculty. I had to make my living playing the saxophone.

Pater Urbanec went to prison.

At first, Madam Editor came to see us almost every day seeking encouragement. Everything in the factory offended her. Vulgar jokes, immoral talk, coarse and dull work. "It's so mechanical, Doctor, so mechanical! There is absolutely no need for thought! And all my life I've worked with my mind!"

She was being broken into the job by an oldish foreman, a widower, who called her "girl" and made indecent proposals to her, such as inviting her out to the movies or to dances. Let's live a little, he'd say to her.

The Editor's horror knew no bounds.

Then Julie's older sister Tereza married a Protestant. Madam Editor kept wringing her hands and spent a week in churches (after work), kneeling and praying for poor Terezinka.

Some time later, I was sent to jail for two weeks for committing light physical damage, under the influence of alcohol, upon a certain youth who kept pawing Julie in places of her body that were out of bounds. When I got out, Madam Editor warned me that alcohol is bad for the health and arouses animal instincts, though in my case its effect was rather the opposite.

Strangely enough, I noticed that she didn't say a word about the soul or about morality.

Half a year later, Communist Youth member Pavel Nedochodil was elected as the Party's candidate. Madam Editor—whose visits to Papa Nedochodil had become much rarer—came one evening, and seemed to take the news in stride. For a while, she chatted about nothing in particular and then got on the subject of the factory, the need to understand those people, who actually aren't a bad sort, it's true they use immoral expressions but this is due to the fact that they had been deprived of a good education.

She didn't add "during the first, bourgeois republic," the standard phrase used by *Rudé Právo,* because she didn't dare go quite that far in the presence of Papa Nedochodil. I noticed that she wore a new dress, modestly high in front but at the same time quite close-fitting so that her bosom clearly outlined the space intended for it. Whatever she was like, Madam Editor certainly aroused sinful ideas. She also wore nylon stockings with black seams and white high-heeled shoes. She told us that the foreman—that widower—heehee—kept hinting that the two of them ought to get hitched—he says—heehee—he needs a good woman. He says a man without a woman is no man at all.

Of course, she doesn't take any of that too seriously. But on her birthday he bought her—heehee—a handbag. An awful one, of course. He's got real low-brow taste. She didn't want to accept it, but he insisted and yesterday he even brought her—heehee—a bouquet of forget-me-nots . . .

After that, she stopped coming to Papa Nedochodil.

We heard various rumors.

We learned that she had moved in with that foreman and lived with him in one nest, as the expression goes.

And that she was getting active in the revolutionary workers' movement.

After that—well, after that there was no longer any interest in her at Papa Nedochodil's house.

Some more time passed, and in general I was getting along fine. I played tenor sax, and even had some female admirers.

I had a few smashing suits hanging in my closet, found a luxurious sublet on Rajský Hill in a villa of a former composer of hit songs for the Tyláček operetta company (who had made a timely switch to military marches and workers' choruses). I broke up with Miss Julie Nedochodil, who went on to marry a refrigerator repair man; and all in all, socialism suited me just fine.

One Sunday afternoon, in summer, as we were playing for a huge crowd in the Fučík Park of Rest and Relaxation, my throat was getting parched and during our break I got into line in front of a watermelon stand.

The attendant kept slicing the watery spheres with a rusty knife and slid the sections down a bare plank, where swarms of flies gaily copulated in the pink juice.

"Comrade!" I heard someone in back of me say, "Comrade! You ought to cover those boards with something, at least some wrapping paper! This is terribly unhygienic! And as a food handler you ought to wear a white coat! Not a sweaty shirt . . . It's not fair to your fellow comrades, comrade, to give them spoiled goods for their honestly earned money!"

I turned around.

My eyes nearly popped out of my head. I beheld a large, shining, five-point red star on the lapel of a modest yet elegant tailored dress.

In the dress stood Madam Editor.

I was sporting a jazzy white jacket and the hitch from my tenor sax was looped around my neck.

I thought it wiser to remain anonymous.

What applies to all the members of a given class,
is true of each of them individually.

SYLLOGISTIC AXIOM

Take certain set phrases and expressions, like: "You made your bed, now lie in it." Or: "A man makes his own luck." When I hear such stuff, I could explode. Or things like: "Nation X is incensed by the behavior of Nation Y." Seriously, what kind of nonsense is that? Or: "The assembly unanimously approved . . ."

Unanimously. It would be interesting to find out what the various members really thought, if somebody could see inside their brains and write it up.

But nobody ever will. I tend to think that the world will always have its secret police, and consequently there will always be private opinions and unanimously approved opinions.

Not to mention so-called common-sense opinions.

Alas, ideal society, ideal society! What turns dream into nonsense? Why will nobody ever see you come into being? Why are you as unattainable as a perpetual motion machine?

Of course, I shall never proclaim such thoughts publicly. I'm not that crazy.

As you know, ladies, the people who fare best in this world are usually the worst bastards. And if you insist on proof, you can kiss my you-know-what. Pardon me.

The only excuse for your naivete is the reformed school curriculum and the resulting ignorance of classical Greek. You don't even know what an axiom is. An axiom is a basic, completely self-evident judgment that confirms itself and needs no further proof.

In order to keep that definition firmly in your head, just remember this example of an axiom: the people who fare best in this world are usually the worst bastards.

These bastards are generally the most ardent proclaimers of truths. Truths don't bother them. Truths never knock them out or shake their guts.

Pardon me.

Let me give you just one such story about truth.

It happened at a time before they kicked me out of English and American Studies. I had volunteered to help out in the American Institute and in Friends of the USA, and I worked like a demon, not out of any love for capitalism—I had no strong feelings about that—but because I was bucking for a grant or fellowship that would enable me to visit that imperialist country and take in the likes of Mary Lou Williams with my own eyes and ears.

So when Uncle Sam's army decided to arrange weekly visits to Prague for its soldiers stationed in Pilsen, I volunteered to accompany them as an interpreter.

Like everything else, it was fun at first and then it became a bore. To drag twenty gum-chewing Yanks, Saturday after Saturday, to churches from four to eight, or to cafes from eight to midnight—those were our shifts—and to listen to the same old stuff: Say, ain't you people never heard of Coke machines? Hey, get a loada this church! Simply gorgeous! Oh yeah, gorgeous! And those same old questions, like a phonograph stuck in a groove: Say, don't you mind you've got them Ruskies over here? Hey, what the hell are you, anyway—a communist or a democrat?

Believe me, I heard enough of that kind of stuff in my department, where even pretty girls were possessed by politics and anybody who didn't belong to some party was fair game for proselytizing. They even wrestled for you in a literal sense of the word—Šiska the Social Democrat actually tore my jacket trying to yank me out of the grasp of a certain Populist. As for me—well, I was simply at a loss what to think about it all, in other words it was all too confusing. And so I joined the Gramophone Club.

In short, ladies, as you've no doubt gathered, I was an idealistic simpleton and I should have known quite clearly what to join and what to think. Or at least, I should have kept saying aloud that I think it.

But I'm an idiot.

I was born that way, and I'll stay that way.

It's incurable.

Even nowadays, although I've knocked around the world a bit and learned how to make the right faces and the right sounds, sometimes I still get so mad that I feel like screaming: Leave me alone! I haven't got any political convictions! I am nothing, I think nothing, I don't know—honestly, I simply don't know who is right and what's what! Yes, if you insist, I can declare unambiguously that you are right, but as far as my private opinion is concerned, I simply don't know. I don't know, and that's that! Leave me alone! I do my work, I blow my tenor sax night after night as well as I know how, just like that fellow over there, Bull Mácha, spends his days running a lathe to make an honest living. Why did you kick him out of the Bulvárka for dancing "in a provocative way," when there is no such a law? Why don't you let him wear his ducktail and walk on three-inch platforms if that's what gives him pleasure, him and his chick who also does an honest day's work, in the *Rudé Právo* canteen, of all places.

Never mind, excuse my nerves. They get the best of me every now and then. Let me return to my theme: those Yanks gave me a pain in the ass, with all their questions.

Pardon me.

I should use three dots, like Krpata.

Every Monday we used to play for the Yanks in the Bulvárka, though in those days it was called Alfa, if you remember. Those Monday evenings were meant to give them a proper send-off before they returned to their bases.

That's when I made my fateful blunder.

It was like this: the Yanks had just finished an infantile folk dance, we blew a few notes for them from sheet music they had brought with them, and they returned to their tables, all heated up. We took a break, I got up, and then I spotted one soldier, his name was Bob or Seymour or something like that, and this soldier—who was a real political nut—was motioning at me to come over. He was beckoning so insistently that I willy-nilly set out for his table—but when I saw who was sitting there with him I dropped the nilly and became all willy.

You see, it was a woman!

But what a woman!

Like an ad for Max Factor makeup and a Maidenform brassiere.

A joy to behold!

Bob-or-Seymour introduced me right away and the Yankee enchantress trilled a hawaya in a honeyed alto voice, her teeth pearling, her dimples dimpling, her Scarlett O'Hara pupils zeroing in on me—in short, I've never belonged among the nonflammables but at that moment I'd have caught fire had I been made of asbestos.

I stopped perceiving my surroundings and like a sentimental ninny I perceived nothing but her. Her name was Eileen. And she was such a joy.

A joy like . . . well, forget comparisons.

Zetka and the band launched into a boogie-woogie and instead of playing my tenor sax I sat next to Eileen and couldn't pry myself away.

In a daze, I asked her for a dance.

I'm sorry, I don't dance. Excuse me, she said, and it sounded like a Mellophone or another such instrument with an equally melodious name.

And so we just sat there and chatted.

God knows what about. I believe we talked about music, about jazz, symphonies, operas, which she said she adored. I have the impression we also talked about the Bird and the Duke but also about Aaron Copland, Darius Milhaud, Frederick Delius and I praised them all because she adored them, although I would have been hard-pressed if I had to spell some of those names.

I'm not going into long descriptions, but it must be so clear to you ladies that it was love at first sight and thus the best thing that can happen to a human being on this earth.

Because nothing else in the world is worth a shit.

Pardon me.

But there you have another axiom, ladies.

I floated on clouds of enchantment and felt blissful; I don't think I had felt that blissful before, except perhaps with Geraldine, but that's another story. This was different, a sweet promise, a marshmallow that wasn't going to cloy or melt away or turn gooey.

And then . . .

I had already written Zetka off that evening. When Lexa came to fetch me, I told him to let Zetka know that I was through for the night and that they should manage with three saxophones. Lexa interpreted that to mean that I was struck by an attack of cardiac intoxication. And the band played for us a jazzed-up version of "Love, Sweet Love."

Ah, yes. In those days the band still had a sense of humor, they pulled real jokes, not just phony gags to amuse the public. Later, Harry and Lexa got locked up for trying to cross the border, and that was the end of the band and of the jokes.

I tried a few more times to lure Eileen onto the dance floor, but each time she gave me a warm smile and said: No thank you, I really don't dance. And then: Please stop asking me. I've already told you, I don't dance. And when at last her face shrank into an angry grimace with two wrinkles at the root of her nose, I stammered: Excuse me, excuse me, please!

Bob-or-Seymour seemed to have evaporated or changed his form or dissolved in alcohol, in a stein of beer I guess, because that was the only kind of alcohol served in the joint.

Truly, I had no idea what happened to him.

And don't get the notion that I had only dreamed him up. When I first entered the place, he was really there and he really spoke to me.

And then he simply vanished.

It's a fact.

And all of a sudden, while the band was on a break, the smooth Yankee cooing of endearing words that seemed to flow effortlessly from my lips was interrupted by a racket from the outside.

Eileen turned her profile to me, the gilded letter

"U.S." on the lapels of her uniform glistened, the red heart hanging from a multicolored ribbon took on a ruby sheen.

And fool that I was, I took it for some sort of jewelry!

On a uniform!

My only excuse was the fact that in addition to my normal, natural idiocy, love had made me into an even bigger fool.

Look, Eileen said. I turned to the window. Out in the street I saw a procession, a sea of red banners and portraits of Stalin of the kind painted by artistically gifted schoolchildren who have a progressive-minded teacher.

How can you stand it? Eileen asked. I felt as if I had been stabbed. Again, politics. And this morning star, this Venus, this new constellation had to bring up politics!

Stand what? I said.

Don't you people have any national pride? she said. How can you walk around carrying flags of a foreign country? Your own flag is completely lost among them, if it's there at all, she said, watching the procession.

Eileen, please, can't we drop the subject?

But this interests me, she said with determination, and two wrinkles formed above her nose. That upset me. OK, I said.

It interests me. I can't understand it. She spoke in that twangy American English of hers, which would probably give a British aristocrat heart failure but which made my native language seem like the speech of peasants. In such situations, a foreign language always has that kind of effect.

I said to Eileen: National pride has nothing to do with it. It's a matter of gratitude.

I perpetrated one of the truths.

Eileen's eyes opened wide: Gratitude?

Yeah, I said. The Russians liberated us, and we're grateful.

But that's silly, Eileen answered. We were attacked just like they were, except it was the Japanese, and so we went to war, too. Why don't you carry American flags? Or British? Or French?

We do.

Where? Where are they? Look! Not a single one.

I looked, but of course quite unnecessarily. In a procession of this sort they obviously weren't going to wave any stars and stripes.

Eileen lectured me: The war was won by the Allies. Some of them cleaned out one country, others another. That depended on the strategic and tactical situation and geographic location. She spoke like a handbook for officer cadets. So if you must show gratitude, you should carry flags of the U.N.

Oh, please, can't we drop this subject? Let's dance!

She blanched a little, those two wrinkles reappeared

over her nose. Don't you understand English? I do not dance! She seemed rather irritated.

Pardon me, I said quickly.

She kept on insisting: Answer me! She leaned her elbows on the table. On a finger of her alabaster hand there was an aquamarine ring. She was probably no rich American, certainly not, otherwise she wouldn't be a WAC corporal. But she was a beautiful American.

Fragrant as coconut milk.

Why are you doing things like that? Why are you doing it? I know the standard answer, but what is the real reason?

What do you mean? I pretended not to understand.

Those Russian flags. Why do you have all those Russian flags all over the place?

Instead of saying what I truly thought, I uttered a truth.

Perhaps it was because I had been hearing it everywhere, or perhaps because I liked to tease Americans with Bolshevik slogans when they got on my nerves.

I uttered a truth. And I uttered it in the proper classical *pluralis majestaticus.*

Listen, I said. I know that other nations were involved in the war besides Russia. But people simply feel the greatest gratitude to those who have shed the most blood for them. And that was the Russians. Yes, we know that America deserves credit for victory, we don't deny it. But America gave material aid, tanks, planes, ships, whereas the Russians gave their blood.

That's as far as I got. I suddenly noticed that Eileen was no longer sitting, but standing. The Russians gave blood, she said, and her voice was trembling. The Russians gave blood and the Americans tanks. You . . . you . . . you stupid bastard! she said, all excited. The Russians blood and Americans guns, she said, the red heart trembling on her chest, and all of a sudden there was an explosion in front of my eyes, stars streamed around my head and I saw Lexa choking on the podium right in the middle of a solo.

I shook my head and realized I'd been slapped.

Amid the falling stars I saw Eileen indignantly walking away.

I watched her saucily short, reddish hair under her cap, the smooth, neatly fitting back of her uniform, the curve of her slender behind, the legs . . .

Yes, dear Lord, you'll probably never forgive me, and even if you do, old softie that you are, I'll still keep kicking myself for the rest of my life.

Here I'd been dishing up one truth after another, like a candidate for public office, and it turned out that she simply couldn't dance with me. Only an acrobat could dance with that kind of prosthesis for a leg.

Since that time I can't bear truths.

I know, maybe a truth becomes Truth only *en gros. En*

détail it's at most a *lèse majesté*. But still, it gives me a pain in
the . . . , to use the three-letter word so favored by Krpata.

Pardon me, ladies.

Don't think me rude.

There's nothing in the world ruder than truths.

A Case For Political Inspectors

We believe in man, in his infinite
capacity for development.

Dalibor Pecháček:

OF CLASS CONSCIOUSNESS

There are various reasons why people become "progressive."

Some do it out of hunger and misery.
Others, out of intellectual convictions.
Some do it for the sake of careers.
And some, because they shit in their pants.

The latter was the reason our good Judge Bohadlo progressed in such a progressive fashion, may the Good Lord bless his soul.

Actually, this is one more story about Political Inspectors, individuals entrusted with guarding socialist values and checking people's political correctness. It is a story about watchfulness and vigilance. And though no PI's appear here directly, they hover in the background and are present in spirit.

When I first had the honor of meeting Judge Bohadlo, he turned out to be a well-preserved, elderly gentleman. A kindly looking chubby fellow, with delicate, rosy cheeks that bespoke fine meals and choice wines, delicate rosy hands that had never known manual labor, a round little belly and a mouth shining like Klondike gold.

A flat in a modern apartment house, a spouse bedecked with bracelets, an aristocratic little dog—as solid a couple as a Biedermeier chair or a table at the Hotel Ambassador.

A district judge or something of the sort, I didn't

know his exact title but certainly a few ranks above the ordinary. His schoolmate was the father of my former girlfriend Julie Nedochodil, and it was at the Nedochodils that I had the honor.

In precommunist days, he used to visit there once in a while, when he had some business to discuss with Papa Nedochodil. After 1945, he formed some sort of connection with cloisters, church organizations and the Catholic Populist party.

He had already been involved in politics before the war, but in those days he was connected with the Agrarian party.

After discussions in Papa Nedochodil's study, Madam Nedochodil would invite them to the dining room for a bit of refreshment, and there they sat, sipped wine from South-Moravian cloisters and munched on sandwiches spread with goat cheese from East-Slovakian cloisters, while Judge Bohadlo recounted tales from the good old golden days.

He especially liked to recall the fox hunts on the estates of Prince Schwarzenberg and Baron Simmenthal. But his dearest friend was Count Humprecht Gelenj, who entered the Premonstratian Order in 1945.

The judge made no secret of his distaste for communism.

And so they lived, grew obese and enjoyed themselves.

In February 1948, the ground under Judge Bohadlo's feet suddenly gave way, but he grasped the support held out to him and performed a grandiose somersault.

He applied for membership in the Communist party.

And what's more—he was accepted.

And so Judge Bohadlo became a communist.

Naturally, this triggered difficult inner struggles.

Seeking relief for his spiritual torments, he turned to Papa Nedochodil for moral support.

He tried to justify himself:

First of all, he is unused to physical work. Suppose they fired him, what then?

Secondly, he supports a sick wife, who needs spa treatments.

And thirdly, somebody's got to stick it out, to save what can be saved.

This third, heroic sounding argument met with Papa Nedochodil's halfhearted approval.

But the big blow was still to come. The pope issued an excommunication decree.

And he really let them have it.

Excommunication applied to all members of the Communist party, as well as any person aiding the communist movement directly or indirectly (reading communist books and newspapers, listening to communist broadcasts, etc., etc.).

In other words, in Czechoslovakia, it applied to practically everybody.

Above all, of course, to Party members.

For a long time, Judge Bohadlo failed to come to Papa Nedochodil's house. Then one day he appeared. His pink second chin drooped lifelessly, his pince-nez kept dropping off his nose.

Somebody, he said in a shaky voice, has to stick it out, save what can be saved. As long as he remains in inner opposition.

Papa Nedochodil had a rather different opinion and his gaze upon the judge's pale pink cheeks was somewhat disdainful, yet because he was basically a kindly soul he offered his friend such an ingenious construction of *reservatio mentale* as applied to the papal decree that the judge began to see that ominous document in an entirely new light. He gobbled up the roast pork Madam Nedochodil offered him, washed it down with mead, and left in a virtually buoyant mood.

All the same, an evil deed is an evil deed. One can keep on thinking up excuses and seek relief in dialectic logic, but an evil deed gives rise to a bad conscience, and that works night and day.

With a sledgehammer.

Two days later, we had the judge back on our neck. Full of torment, near collapse. Somebody, he whispered, has to stick it out . . .

A new injection of casuistry, combined with almond pastry and mead, put him back on his feet.

He left in much calmer shape.

Two days later, he returned.

Very shaken.

And so it continued, until the mead ran out.

He stopped coming for a long time.

And then one day he suddenly appeared at the door, looking radiant. He announced that he had consulted a confessor.

The confessor had reassured him: Somebody indeed has to stick it out and save what can be saved.

I was rather surprised, but then I discussed the matter with Julie in her room, and that clever girl reconstructed the story this way: Imagine, she said, a clergyman who is in every respect a proper priest, except that the poor fellow lacks the courage of the early Christian martyrs. It's hard to condemn him for that, even in this nation of Hussite heroes. And now somebody walks into his confessional, kneels down and confesses that he sinned by joining the Communist party. What is that poor old fellow to do?

Of course, the matter is clear, according to the papal decree he is forbidden to absolve him as long as he remains in league with the godless brood.

Only . . .

Suppose the penitent is an undercover agent? If I refuse him absolution he may turn me in.

So imagine the situation: the judge is kneeling in the confessional, trembling, gnawed by his bad conscience.

Behind the grating sits the priest, trembling, the ugly thought of prison oppressing his mind.

This mutual trembling, naturally, could only be ended through compromise.

Thesis approved: Somebody's got to stick it out, save what can be saved.

Proviso: The aforementioned somebody must not perform anything evil, and in his heart must continue to oppose those communist ideas that conflict with the teachings of the church.

Please note: "those communist ideas that conflict with the teachings of the church." In other words, not communism as such.

Why not?

Well, because the reverend father was suddenly struck by still another terrible possibility: if that penitent is an informer, he could just as well turn him in for giving absolution as for refusing to give it. After all, what would it mean to absolve someone of communism? That would logically imply that the reverend father considered communism a sin, and that he was guided by the pope rather than by the State Bureau for Religious Affairs.

In short, that poor priest spent some very trying moments in connection with Judge Bohadlo's confession.

The compromise lay uneasy on his conscience, and so

he at least urged the penitent to practice energetically the virtue of Christian charity: concretely, in terms of the judge's profession, he should do his utmost to ease the human lot of the prisoners with whom he came in contact.

This was a program to which Judge Bohadlo responded with the greatest of enthusiasm.

He repeatedly reported to us on his acts of charity:

He smuggled chocolate bars to Miss Skladanovská, daughter of the former senator and friend of my former love Julie Nedochodil, whom he had socked with two years in jail for an attempt at illegal emigration.

He frequently smuggled packages of American vitamins into the cell of Mr. Simms, a former editor whom he had slammed with a fifteen-year sentence.

After meting out a life sentence to a certain wholesale merchant, the judge patted him on the back and whispered in his ear: Keep up your spirits, friend!

Whereupon that malcontent answered in a loud voice: Shut your trap, you swine!

Ingratitude rules the world. Dr. Bohadlo performed his good deeds without thought of reward, like a true scout.

He would recount these stories to us, always managing to add his denunciation of communist legal and investigative methods, and he let us in on some unbelievably sensational details of political trials.

A bad conscience turned the judge into an ideal source of juicy information.

The Voice of America would have paid me for them in gold.

But I have always followed the principle: freedom is better than riches.

And it's paid off for me so far.

The judge kept cursing communism like the prophet Habakuk, for reasons best known to himself, while furiously munching on hors d'oeuvres and pastry. His eyes burned with indignation. In those moments his conscience grew calmer. But then he'd leave for a street rally or the meeting of some organization where he'd excoriate the imperialists, and his bad conscience stuck out its horns.

At Papa Nedochodil's, of course, he tried as hard as he could to ridicule such proceedings. After indoctrination sessions where they discussed dialectical and historical materialism, he declared (at Papa Nedochodil's): I've forgotten more of this nonsense than they will ever learn. I recognized it for trash when I was still a young puppy like you, he added, turning to me.

He said it in the heat of the moment, so I didn't take offense. I understood him.

But that didn't help.

They promoted him.

His wife won approval for sojourn in a spa, whereas the wife of an impoverished shoemaker in the judge's basement, who stubbornly insisted on remaining a private entrepreneur, was rejected.

Does that surprise you? You don't seem to understand: Judge Bohadlo was politically sound. A working member of the intelligentsia.

Whereas the shoemaker? Suppose they gave him a bit of leeway. In no time at all, he'd hire apprentices and start exploiting the working class. People of his type are incorrigible. Petty entrepreneurs are the germs of capitalism.

Judge Bohadlo thus became an ever higher jurist and in the end an instructor of political education.

He stuck it out, that's true, and saved what could be saved.

In the single year of 1950 he smuggled in 28 packages of American chocolate, 5 kilos of vitamins, 3 kilos of sugar, 2,000 cigarettes, 18 books for reading and 22 prayer books.

He kept precise records, including name, date, type of merchandise and quantity.

In excoriating the Communist party he reached a McCarthyite level of intensity.

And so it continued.

What's that?

You're asking whether he's still a high judge? Whether they ever unmasked him and got rid of him?

But my dears, you are so naive!

Of course, obviously, naturally. In the end, our society always gets rid of its internal enemies, even if they managed to lead it by the nose for years. Our society has eliminated—and continues to eliminate—all parasites who believe they can hide behind slogans and phrases and conceal their foul schemes.

Judge Bohadlo?

Of course our society got rid of him in the end.

How?

He died.

A stroke.

Say what you like, death is still the best Political Inspector.

How They Got Nabbed

Everything that happens,
happens by necessity.

Democritus

I hear they let Hiram C. Nutsbellow out, on account of good behavior. OK, I really have nothing against it. I've never had anything against Hiram C. Nutsbellow. But are they going to let Licátko out, too? That's what I'd really like to know. Because I'll bet Licátko is on his best behavior. He has never been anything but a well-behaved, quiet, inconspicuous hipster, the kind you see on Saturday nights puking at street corners of downtown Prague.

I have this feeling that although Nutsbellow might be out, Licátko shouldn't hold his breath. Sure, he's been in longer than Nutsbellow, but Nutsbellow is a Somebody. I mean Nutsbellow is like hard currency, a valuable item of trade. And Licátko? Few people know that he even exists.

Maybe Sylvie still does. Then again, maybe even she no longer cares.

Actually, when I think about it, I've never had much to do with Licátko. He was a very close-mouthed hipster. Now, take Paul Rameš, his mouth never took a rest. He was a born announcer and commentator. He won't be coming out so very soon. I just can't imagine him behaving good.

It's all a matter of character. Rameš was a vibes player and most vibes players have been born on a funny farm. Paul Rameš certainly was a nut. At one time he played with us in Krinolin, that was when vibes came back into style and before they put the kabosh on bebop. He was never a wheeler-dealer, he just tried to make a little extra because he had a wife and a kid whom he drowned in puppy love. Not that the fat treasure of his deserved it, candy and loafing had turned her into a horizontal giant, she wasted whole days glued to a park bench or gobbling it up with her hen friends at the Myšák Coffee House. Well, Paul was simply a nut.

During the day he worked for News Limited, the outfit that later became so notorious. He was terribly happy there. When he heard that I was thrown out of Anglo-American Studies because I was under suspicion of believing in God, he tried to talk me into joining up with them. You jerk, he used to say, staring at me with his crossed eyes, five thou for five hours a day, as much chewing gum as you can stuff in your mouth and now and again some used but great-looking threads from Nutsbellow—and besides, from time to time there is a chance for a bit of unofficial business, if you know what I mean—he would add, winking with his crossed eyes and grinning like a moron, the way he did when pounding the vibes. Screw Zetka. Two or three sessions a week with them should be enough to keep you solvent. He showed me a dirty, well-worn shirt inherited from Nutsbellow, and gave me a package of gum. Come and join us, you jerk, the boss asked me to keep on the lookout for a good man.

And so I went to look the joint over. They had their offices in Kabert Street. Leather club chairs, pinup girls and incredibly endowed strippers on the walls, quiet as a churchyard except for the back room, where teletypes gently clicked while a leather-clad hipster sipped a glass of whiskey, feet propped on desk and syphon in hand.

Licátko.

We barely exchanged three words of greeting, something like hi . . . hi . . . ahoy, and then I glanced at the beat-up teletype. A tape was just sliding out of it.

Paul picked it up, and his crossed eyes twinkled with amusement. I glanced over his shoulder and saw the word MINDZENTI. And words like FRAMEUP and COMMUNIST TRIAL.

You've got it pretty nice here, I said, looking around. I noticed that the hipster was quietly giving me the once-over.

And what fun! Paul said. You wanna see how we get our kicks?

Sure, I answered.

All right, watch this! Paul sat at the teletype, thought for a moment and then reached into the keyboard. I read over his shoulder:

(PRAGUE) TERROR IN THE STREETS. A MAN JUMPED OUT OF A TROLLEY CAR ON WENCESLAS SQUARE JUST AS IT WAS TURNING THE CORNER AT THE NATIONAL MUSEUM. AT THAT MOMENT TWO MEN CARRYING AN ENORMOUS PORTRAIT OF STALIN PASSED THE CAR AND THE UNFORTUNATE TRAVELER FLEW THROUGH THE PAINTING LEAVING A BIG HOLE BETWEEN THE RUSSIAN DICTATOR'S EYES. THE MAN WAS SEIZED ON THE SPOT BY TWO HEAVILY ARMED POLICE-

MEN, CRUELLY BEATEN, HURLED UNCONSCIOUS INTO A PA-
TROL WAGON AND DRIVEN AWAY. NOTHING IS KNOWN
ABOUT HIS FURTHER FATE.

As Paul finished typing and the tape vanished into the
machine, to reappear somewhere among our foreign enemies, Licátko burst into laughter.

That's great, I said.

And backed out of there as quickly as I could.

I suppose this world needs a few idealists. But I've
never counted myself as one of them.

Then official lightning struck several times in rapid
succession as far as jazz and bebop were concerned, and
some drunk sat down on top of Paul's vibes. We barely
managed to scrape up a few gigs in the few joints left for
the non–builders of socialism. I lost track of Paul. He did
meet me a couple of times and tried to talk me into joining
up with Nutsbellow; he enticed me with trousers made
over from American officers' pinks, cartons of Chester-
fields and a pornographic magazine with stereoscopic
glasses that made the pictures burst right out of the page.
But I was wary and chose to pretend that I was lazy and
liked to sleep during the day.

Then Rameš disappeared completely. Instead, I
bumped into Licátko, under rather remarkable circumstances.

One Thursday, when our usual joints were closed, the
band made an outing to Sázava, to the summer place of a

cat named Davida. Spring was just starting to tune up, the village looked like a ghost town, everything still locked up and boarded up, and just about the only thing that moved were patches of fog rolling over the water.

And suddenly, who trots out of the neighboring cottage if not Licátko, in gardening pants with white stitching and cotton suspenders like they wear in the States, and right behind him who comes hopping out into the fresh air but a blonde looker, a blonde so gorgeous that our eyes turned downright astigmatic.

Behind me Davida whistled through his teeth.

Licátko smiled shyly and said hi.

The looker realized that she was in deshabille and withdrew.

We, too, went inside and Davida sat down on his bunk.

Gentlemen, he said, this beats Sodom!

What do you mean? You know those cats? I asked.

You bet! said Davida. That's Licátko of Licátko and Co., bathroom accessories. And that relic of bourgeois taste is his mother.

So what? said Ríša. He is spending the weekend with his mother, that's all.

And that indeed turned out to be the case. That night, we lay on our bunks, the room dark except for the glow of cigarettes as Davida explained Licátko's history. Our neighbors' windows were lit up and we could hear the sounds of Glen Miller and Stan Kenton. This, in brief, was the story:

Licátko's old man owned a factory manufacturing bathtubs and bidets. He married a Russian émigré who bestowed on him Licátko Junior. At the time of the communist takeover she died of a stroke. A couple of months ago dad married again and the rosebud presently being entertained by Kenton's mellow tones was the bathtub king's second wife. She was two years Licátko Junior's junior.

Davida fell silent. Then he got up, and gazed for a long time at the windows of the neighboring cottage, their brightness now dimmed by shades.

By sheer coincidence, I kept running into them. The very next Sunday we met at the races, and Licátko introduced his stepmother to me. Her name was Sylvie. Close up, after talking to her a bit, she didn't have that dynamic impact, but in a way that was to her advantage. She came across as a quiet, nice kid, as sweet on the eyes as a sunset in the Tatras and as pleasing on the ear as the sounds of a glass harmonica when you're resting in an easy chair at a resort hotel after a first-rate dinner.

A veritable music of the spheres.

And she was tailor-made for Licátko. Silent, unassuming, clean, neat. An American type.

She had a perfect class background: she came from a proletarian family, and was an orphan to boot. She didn't have much schooling, started working as a salesgirl at the

White Swan, but the pay was so miserable that she switched to a factory job.

The factory turned out to be Licátko and Co., enameled bathroom fixtures.

One day, the owner of the factory saw her enameling a bidet, and started to smolder.

Soon he caught fire.

He was the one that turned her into an American looker. But when you got to know her personally, she remained nice and unassuming and proletarian. I mean that as words of praise.

But I'd better not think about it too much.

That day at the races I began to sense what Licátko was all about, and at the same time the signal of an unpleasant premonition began blinking in my head.

Licátko bet stubbornly all afternoon. He circled the bookmakers' booths like a hawk around sparrows, he kept making notes, counting, figuring. By the time the horses stopped running he was ahead by a hundred crowns. He bought Sylvie a bouquet of tulips and a bunch of radishes.

And so it went, Sunday after Sunday. And then? Well, it ended the way it had to end, the way everything ends.

Badly.

Licátko had practically turned into the phantom of the turf. He haunted the first floor at Juliš where they bet on foreign races. In the summer he spent every Sunday in

Karlsbad, in the spring and fall at the Chuchle track. Always with notebook and pencil in hand, taciturn, eyebrows knitted in concentration, Sylvie, elegant and vivacious, always beside him.

They were such a classical hipster pair, the very Platonic idea of hipsterdom, that I was ready to bawl with sheer happiness every time I saw them.

A joy forever, as Keats would say.

Except that Licátko went broke, started pawning his overcoats and other objects, and after a while there was nothing left in his flat except pawn tickets.

He thought of trying his hand at translating. In those days there was still a shortage of people who could read Cyrillic texts, and so Licátko, who inherited some Russian from his mother, offered his services.

They were accepted, and Licátko was given *The Victory of Collective Farmer Vadim* for translation.

For a time, Paul filled in for him at the News Limited teletype desk, and Licátko translated the collective farmer's progressive opinions. But it was no use. In no time at all he squandered his advance and the track kept gobbling up one pawn ticket after another.

He pawned Nutsbellow's Underwood.

"You crazy? What in the world are you gonna tell him?" I said, when we accidentally happened to meet in the pawnshop.

He smiled sheepishly and shrugged his shoulders.

They gave him quite a decent sum for the Underwood and he was off to Juliš.

By the sunset the sum was gone.

Soon thereafter everything caved in on him, like a rain of left and right hooks on a punch-drunk boxer.

At home, his dad found out about his affair with Sylvie.

Nutsbellow discovered that his Underwood, wall clock and oil painting of President Truman were in hock. With a shy smile, Licátko offered him the pawn tickets.

In front of his dad, too, Licátko appeared genuinely contrite, but that didn't stop the former factory owner from giving Junior a few hefty smacks.

On Sylvie her husband made use of a bullwhip.

She cried, and Licátko was incensed. Miraculously, he found himself a small flat and moved out of the family house. Sylvie moved in with him, but Licátko Senior refused a divorce and so they lived in sin.

Actually, that was hard to believe, because they both looked so innocent.

Hiram C. Nutsbellow behaved like a true gentleman, or at least so it seemed to me at the time. He redeemed the pawned items himself and even gave Licátko a raise.

I thought—jerk that I was—that it was on account of his social consciousness. On account of Sylvie and so on.

I was simply a jerk. A triple-crowned idiot.

Licátko gradually got his belongings out of hock and

started furnishing a home. First he redeemed his silver cocktail shaker, then his tuxedo, an ivory mahjong set, and a Chinese screen with somewhat juicy depictions (which they had at first rejected on the grounds that socialist pawnshops do not accept pornography, but then relented on account of its quality material). All these things were now safely back in the apartment, along with Sylvie in toreador pants ensconced in the kitchen corner. She had quit the bidet factory as soon as she became Madam Licátko, and after her husband had slammed the door on her she had to look for other work.

This time it was easier. She worked at what she was born for. She became a fashion model.

Now she hopped about happily in the kitchen nook, draped in a pink apron with the inscription KISS ME, HUBBIE!, while in another corner Licátko pounded the typewriter.

When I think of that blissful domestic scene I could bawl like a whore.

The relationship that developed between Licátko and me was kind of strange. Maybe it was because I continued to have this inkling that the whole thing was destined for a rotten end. I don't know why, I simply had that feeling. Whenever I saw them living like two lovebirds from an ad in *Ladies Home Journal* I felt a pang of the blues and waited for new troubles.

And I was right.

But before the disaster I met once more with Paul
Rameš. That very same day that *The Victory of Collective
Farmer Vadim* came out, the book that Licátko translated
and that paid for their new vacuum cleaner.

I ran into Paul under the Libeň viaduct. He was
wearing a bricklayer's shirt and overalls, and I was afraid
he'd gotten fired from his cushy job. No way, he reassured me, News Limited is beyond the reach of Political
Inspectors. He was still with them, working there till noon
and then moonlighting on a construction job in the afternoon. Just like the USA. The pay in the office is small,
there are few gigs for vibes players, and bricklayers make
good money.

But we're doing OK, he explained, zeroing his
crossed eyes into the distance behind me. Nutsbellow
drops a gift parcel our way now and again, recently I got a
suit, a bit used but made of Harris tweed, occasionally a
few cartons of Chesterfield land on my desk, but that's the
one thing Nutsbellow is pretty stringent about, he doesn't
want to tangle with people's democratic laws.

Natch, said Paul. You bet, I answered.

Why don't you come up with me to the house, he said.
You haven't been to see us since the flood.

So I went with him.

At the house sat the horizontal Mrs. Paul, devouring a
larger-than-life chocolate rabbit, an item either imported
or meant only for export. This one came wrapped in fancy

green foil, too fancy for our circumstances. The child named Ellen was playing with a velvet monkey, and who sat there in a leather jacket if not Licátko! Next to him sat another cool cat looking like a hit man from a gangster movie, with a jacket to match.

They stood up when we entered.

This is Bubeník, the murderer, said Licátko with a shy smile.

The cool cat grinned under his mustache. Mrs. Rameš wagged her finger at Licátko. Paul Rameš burst into laughter.

Hi, I said, shaking the cat's hand. I felt strange.

There followed some conversation about arranging the details. I gathered that whatever he was going to do, he would do it in the West.

Fine goings on, I thought to myself, may the Lord have mercy on us, and I turned to Mrs. Rameš, who offered me a bite of her chocolate rabbit.

Little Ellen had just torn the monkey's head off, licked the sawdust inside and started bawling.

Fortunately, it was getting late and I hurriedly made my farewells.

The cat in the jacket again rose politely to his feet, shook my hand and again grinned under his mustache.

I felt extremely uncomfortable.

Then, as usually happens in such cases, one two three, left hook, right hook, uppercut, KO.

The radio announces that they've picked up Hiram C. Nutsbellow.

I rush to Licátko's place. Sylvie in tears. They picked up Licátko.

As I gallop down the stairs, I pass two strange-looking guys with hats pulled down over their eyes.

I pause in the hallway, and sure enough: after a few moments, lots of crying. They nab Sylvie.

I jump in a taxi and I'm off for Kabert Street. I can't get poor Sylvie out of my mind, my head is spinning with crazy plans for helping her.

I get to Kabert Street just in time to see Paul Rameš being dragged to the paddy wagon, fighting all the way. They manage to shove him in. Terror in the street. Just the way he dreamed it up on the teletype message.

Let's get away from here, I tell the cabbie.

In the evening I stayed home, glued to the radio. Not a word over Radio Prague, but plenty from The Voice of America: "Prague," I made out the announcer's voice over the crackle of jamming. "The communist police today arrested the director of the News Limited press agency, Hiram C. Nutsbellow. Hiram C. Nutsbellow is being accused of espionage. Paul Rameš, an employee of the agency, sent us this afternoon the following teletype message: 'Today at two o'clock, director Nutsbellow and editor Licátko were dragged off by the police. This message is a warning to the Free World. No matter what happens, we shall remain firm, faithful to freedom and democracy.' Our attempts to establish contact with editor Paul Rameš have so far remained fruitless. It seems that his dire prediction came true. Dear listeners, join us to honor in our thoughts these heroes of democracy."

That's what they said.

You have to hand it to Rameš, he may have been a bit of a nut, but he had style.

Something of a hero.

Except that he chose the wrong side. It wasn't his fault. We can choose what we want, but as for wanting what we want . . . there's the rub, as Schopenhauer warned. Freedom of the will doesn't stretch quite that far.

And so they threw the book at them: class enemies, golden youth, scion of an industrialist corrupted by compulsive gambling, relations with the stepmother, sexual perversions—no, actually that was quite a different case, the case of the Mengele brothers—living beyond their means, parasites on society, individuals averse to honest work.

And then, the prosecutor: abetting espionage, supplying slanderous information about the socialist state for the use of enemy propaganda.

Also, giving aid and comfort to Bubeník, a spy and murderer.

The last item made me feel ill. Bubeník had hit some undercover cop over the head and made away with secret documents. They never found him.

A bad show. Sick at heart, I scanned the papers to see how they had dealt with Licátko and Sylvie.

They got the limit. They really gave them the works.

Hiram C. Nutsbellow, twenty-five years.

Paul Rameš, twenty.

Licátko, fifteen.

Sylvie, a year.

When they let her out, she looked just as good as ever, even better, in fact. But she came out with such sad eyes. Went to work in a factory. Tesla, the television outfit.

Licátko Senior, the former industrialist, divorced her while she was still behind bars. He got away with that, because Sylvie had committed a crime against the people's socialist democratic laws.

A few years have now passed, and nowadays Sylvie is once again working as a fashion model. That's good news. And yet, it's still so sad. You see, Sylvie remarried, a designer from the House of Fashion.

And Nutsbellow is out again, while Licátko is still behind bars.

I'll bet he is a model prisoner.

I'm not talking about Paul Rameš. I doubt he is on good behavior. He never was.

But it's different with Licátko.

Now that they swapped that CIA agent Nutsbellow for some bolshie spy, will they take pity on Licátko?

That's what I'd like to know.

Then again, perhaps it's better this way. What would Licátko do, after Sylvie's forgotten all about him? God, what would the poor guy do?

Little Mata Hari of Prague

Society does not consist of the guilty and the innocent,
but of those who have been exposed,
and those who have not yet been exposed.

Insp. Bohuslav Vodička

became acquainted with Geraldine during a party game called "mouth mail" that we were playing at a party celebrating Peter's twentieth birthday. It goes like this: those present sit down around a table alternately by sex, and they pass a wooden matchstick along from mouth to mouth without using their hands. Every time the matchstick has done a turn of the table, a little piece is broken off, so that it is finally just a tiny splinter of a thing, progressing around the table from one player to the next more or less with the aid of the tongue. The one who swallows it or loses it or drops it is required to do some unpleasant task. It can also be played for forfeits, which then turns into a striptease, but unfortunately that didn't happen at Peter's birthday party. It is an unhygienic and interesting game and, unlike other games, has amused everyone with whom I have had occasion to play it, without exception.

And that evening I was in an especially advantageous position, because on my right I had Lizette, and on my left, the girl they had introduced to me as Geraldine, with the face of a first-class Prague ladybird, black hair and black eyes, golden mussels clipped into her little earlobes, in her décolletage a Venetian cameo on a sharp chain, and on her bare arms a collection of gold antiques; her dress was of black taffeta, she smelled of perfumes, and she had a nice mouth, seemingly created for this particular game. And she possessed all that at the age of sixteen and a half.

For me, the evening ended unpleasantly, because I got drunk and barely made it back to where I was to meet the rest of my unit, the Sixth Tank and Self-Propelled Artillery Training Battalion Chorus, with which I had performed the previous afternoon at the plant of the firm that was our patron. I arrived at the Denis railway station a minute after half past four in the morning, undoubtedly in the tow of a guardian angel, who likes to use an alcoholic fog to guide a person safely to his destination, albeit that person had sinned the sin of intemperance and had lost all sense of time and space.

The next day I found a Venetian cameo in the pocket of my uniform jacket.

I tried to recall what had happened, but the only thing that came to my mind were wisps of a few foggy recollections of the Braunšlégr's courtyard and of some indecencies that I had been committing there against Geraldine, primarily with my hands, nothing more than that.

Fortunately, I had another trip to Prague that same week, under the pretext of a medical appointment at the military hospital. As soon as they sent me on my way from the hospital at Strešovice, I headed toward Lizette's. She was a little offended, describing to me in detail my behavior at the party, with a commentary of her own. Her husband Richard, who happened to be home on a six-day pass, because his unit hadn't yet begun to apply the new military regulations for locking soldiers up hermetically within training compounds, also had a commentary, but a different one. The girl called Geraldine was apparently Lizette's brother Pete's girl, according to Lizette. That evening, drunk, I had molested her. I was lucky that Pete had gotten drunk before me so that he never noticed. I had behaved abominably. Said Lizette. On the other hand, her husband said that it wasn't me who had molested the girl, but that she had molested me, because she is a well-known *maîtresse* from the Spořilov district, and Pete is a fool if he doesn't know it. Lizette said that Pete is no fool, and that's just the reason that he is going with Geraldine. To have some fun. And that she's actually not that bad, that it's mostly a lot of talk and gossip. Whereupon Richard declared that clumsy as he is with girls, he wouldn't need more than half an hour to be tête-à-tête etcetera with Geraldine, and Lizette brushed him off contemptuously, how come it took him a year with her, Lizette, and that she'd really like to know how he'd do it with Geraldine in half an hour. Richard replied that she, Lizette, might also be a *maîtresse*—he knew that Lizette would be flattered by that esoteric term—and that's why it took him such an inordinately long time with her; but a *maîtresse* of a different type, and that is how he is prepared to prove his contention in deed, if Lizette is so anxious to see it. And Lizette was furious at how anything so dirty could have occurred to him, considering that he is married, and married in a church at that. I never did find out if it was her Catholic upbringing or just female logic. It was probably a mixture of both.

And so I offered to do the experiment for Richard.

Lizette looked at me suspiciously.

Richard gave me all his support.

"Fine," declared Lizette. "You go there, and in exactly half an hour, I'll ring the bell."

The proof was to be my word of honor.

I went.

Geraldine's family occupied a large apartment on the fifth floor of an apartment building that had belonged to them; at the very top of the building was a little five-sided tower and that is where Geraldine had her own room. The situation was favorable; she opened the door and stared at me, but without much talk or embarrassment she let me in, remarking quickly that she was home alone. She was wearing a blue sweater, a gray skirt and her bare, delicately hairy legs ended in a pair of brown and yellow sandals. She sat down on the couch; above it hung a British Airways map of the world, with British Airways calendars on the walls, along with French reproductions of Victorian prints, and under a photograph of a cheery-looking man with a flower in his buttonhole, with a black mourning ribbon across the corner, was something that surprised me: an empty ammunition belt from a machine gun. And every-where there were plants, vases, figurines, fashion maga-zines from London and Paris, and on the desk an ugly statuette of King Kong, loads of knickknacks and gewgaws, and some red roses on the coffee table, so that the tower room was filled with a sweet fragrance. That fragrance, and all those knickknacks, and black-eyed Geraldine with those gold mussels on her earlobes again—the entire seductive syndrome inspired me to such a degree that I exceeded the prescribed time by seven minutes, and precisely twenty-three minutes after having rung the bell at the door with the brass plate that read Jarmil Kolben, MD, I was lying on the couch with Geraldine, fulfilling the conditions of the experiment.

Lizette was two minutes early, and she rang insistently.

Geraldine got up, annoyed, pulled her skirt back down to her knees, straightened her hair, quickly repaired her lipstick and went to the door. When she left the room, I looked in the mirror and saw I had red smears around my mouth.

I left them there.

It was proof to support my word of honor.

Lizette came in, ran her eyes around the room, and when she saw the smears around my mouth, she blushed a little.

Then, outside, she bawled me out.

But Richard snickered triumphantly.

In essence, Lizette was pleased too. She was hungry for sensations about the girls she knew; she was just upset that I had been the one to prove it.

Because, married or not, she still felt she had proprietary rights to me.

And so that is how I came to know Geraldine fully,
and later I succeeded in finding out her prehistory as well.
Her father had been a patriotic dentist; he fixed teeth at
the Presidential Palace and those of what was left of the
Bohemian aristocracy, exclusively with gold. For that reason he had died an unnatural death during an interrogation at the notorious Gestapo institution that was
commonly known as the Pečkárna during the war. He had
imported Geraldine's mother before the war from Great
Britain. Her name was Genevieve and she was employed by
British Airways, an organization of extreme interest to the
State Security Police. Through her father, Geraldine came
from a family whose prominent member was the famous
nineteenth-century Czech writer Alois Jirásek. Through
her mother, she was descended from an uncertain family
in Soho, noteworthy only for exceptional physical beauty,
and as a result—as Geraldine herself told me with a seductive glance—for a large number of single mothers. Her
own mother was rescued from the traditional fate in her
seventh month as a result of steps taken by the British ambassador at the Presidential Palace in Prague. There were
always some sort of diplomatic troubles surrounding Geraldine.

I visited her again at the closest opportunity, and not
on any instructions from Lizette, but we were left alone

only for a little while—which was enough—and then Pete rushed in, and Geraldine's mama served tea in the dining room; in the course of tea, in order to make an impression on the two ladies, I divulged a number of military secrets, which were especially devoured by Pete Braunšlégr, because the next month he was due to be drafted into military service.

Geraldine was all over him.

Unexpectedly, I was unable to make a date with her.

When Pete went to the bathroom and mama to the kitchen for some fresh tea, I kissed Geraldine, and it seemed to me that she was expecting it.

But she didn't want to make a date.

And then back to Pete, the way she had before.

That confused me.

Later on, of course, I understood, and recognized that for her, it was all as natural as talking and laughing.

She was just that way.

Hard to understand.

And so nothing came of it all, and about three months rolled by. I was no longer a prisoner of the Tank and Artillery Battalion, but an NCO of the highest rank; I harassed rookies and trips to Prague were no problem.

One Saturday when I showed up at Lizette's, horror, confusion and tears reigned.

They had arrested Pete.

They had come for him at his barracks, dragged

him off his bunk, nabbed him with his suitcase and all, and drove him away. He was in jail pending interrogation in České Budejovice, and Geraldine had just left to go there.

I went over to Geraldine's. For the first time mama, with a long cigarette holder, disclosed herself to me. With contempt in her voice, she revealed that they had interrogated Geraldine three times already, but Geraldine had stood firm against those idiots from the secret police and hadn't breathed a word.

What she could have said, I didn't know.

And I didn't ask.

Madame had a strong, penetrating but pleasant voice, and her language was the language of salons, with expressions of the industrial bourgeoisie. She voiced the conviction that no intelligent person could be a communist. I voiced my agreement.

"And would you believe, Doctor," said mama, awarding me the title that I had been prevented from achieving by the postcoup purges, "would you believe that a child like that, Doctor, she isn't seventeen yet, would you believe that they would follow a child like that around and try to get things out of her?"

"No, really?" I wondered.

"Really," said mama. "Such a vulgar fellow, he doesn't even speak Czech right," she said with her English accent, "asking about the people who come here, wanting to know what they talk about, and who it is who comes here, what do you say to that, Doctor?"

"Dreadful," I said.

"But Geraldine sent him packing; I didn't expect that of the girl myself."

"And why did they—" I started to ask.

"You know, British Airways. They've been interested in the local office for a long time, but they didn't liquidate it until a month ago. And people from British Airways used to come here, along with Professor Vašek of the Faculty of Electronics and various people from society—so they were curious, as you can well imagine."

"And where are you working now, Madame?" I said.

"At the Research Institute for Heavy Engineering," she said.

Oh no, I thought to myself.

After six months in jail, Pete was solemnly sentenced to two years of hard labor for undermining troop morale. He had praised American army rations and somebody ratted on him.

Geraldine was harassed about ten times.

Once I was too.

Except that the army is a school of manly virtues. Before they came for me, I was forewarned. First by my driver, who came running into the bowling alley and announced that the secret policeman from division was looking for me down at battalion, and did I want to send a quick message home. I set out for battalion without sending any message. On the way, I was similarly warned by the quartermaster sergeant from the commissary warehouse, three petty officers from battalion and finally by my squad commander, for whom I had been secretly writing reports to present at political schooling sessions.

They didn't want a whole lot from me.

How do I know Peter Braunšlégr and what do I know about his family.

I described all of them as good citizens devoted to the people's democratic regime, and Lizette as a good comrade and friend of Comrade Deputy Director Pitterman. At this point my interrogator interrupted me and asked whether Lizette was my friend as well. Yes, I admitted, but in a different way from Comrade Pitterman. I described Richard as a devoted Communist, and myself as a nonparty Marxist.

After that they didn't bother me anymore.

And after he had served two months, Pete was released as part of an amnesty.

But by the time I got out of the army, everything had changed with Geraldine. True, she sat around with us while Pete described his adventures with interrogation, she was with him morally maybe, and almost certainly, she gratified him erotically after he was set free. But emotionally she was fluttering after an entirely different butterfly— a young man who wore a conical coat with wooden pegs for buttons, a year and a half before that finally became the style in Czechoslovakia too. His name was Paul, he had spent his childhood during the war in neutral Switzerland, he wrote surrealistic prose about the girls he happened to be going with at the time, he was a student at the English high school, and in the end—together with another phony named Bernard, who supported himself by selling penicillin on the black market—they filched two thousand crowns from Geraldine's flat.

After the evening when Pete was released from the clink and came home on a pass, I didn't see Geraldine for a long time. Nor their apartment, full of old-fashioned furniture, with gold jewelry in all sorts of odd drawers that no one in the family had any idea of, so that whenever Lizette wanted to dress up, all she had to do was go over to Geraldine's and inconspicuously borrow something. Nor even that tower room with the British Airways calendars, the ammo belt and the horrendous statuette of King Kong on the desk. Nor mama enveloped in cigarette smoke, with her sarcastic talk about the secret police and communists. Nor even the gold-framed portrait of Master Alois Jirásek that hung in the dining room, with an inscription in faded ink in the master's own hand enjoining someone to *Be a good daughter to your nation!*—someone who couldn't have been Geraldine, first because the master had passed on long before any British ambassadors had called at the Presidential Palace, and second because nobody knows just exactly how it is with nationality in these cases.

When they let me out of the army, I returned to Zetka's jazz band, and I lived under conditions very much in keeping with the people's democracy; at a time when jazz was not encouraged by the powers that be, I hung around the Alfa Cafe, but the situation was gradually improving until Zuzka, our singer, began proclaiming that before the year was out, she would be singing Ella Fitzgerald's repertoire again.

But before the year was out, something else happened first.

Just as I had placed my saxophone in its stand and was getting ready to take a break, a pretty girl stepped up to the bandstand, dressed in a white dress in a floral-print material that you just don't see in Prague, with gold all over her body and with gold mussels on her earlobes.

Geraldine.

She was now over eighteen, and prettier.

We had arranged a date in a minute.

She arrived in a suit straight out of *Vogue* magazine, with a big bow of nylon lace on the front of her blouse, and she twittered on about this and that through until evening. She told me she attends French lessons at the Language Institute mornings, and afternoons she works on some lathe in some small factory that belongs to the People's Co-operative of Toymakers or something. They had turned down her application for the university.

"What do you mean, afternoons? Isn't it afternoon now?"

"It is, but our director is wild about me. Whenever he sees me, his eyes get misty," she said. "I told him I didn't feel well. He always lets me go when I tell him I don't feel well."

"Geraldine, you're a sight for sore eyes," I told her.

She laughed, and told me about mama, about the society people, now for the most part behind bars, about how she has nothing but contempt for people who have no ambitions, that she has ambitions to see the world and be well dressed and learn languages, that is why she works in a factory and her mama lets her keep what she earns to buy her clothes with.

"Damn," I said, looking at her nylon lace, "but you must earn quite a bit. Where did you buy that material?"

"It was a gift," she said and hurriedly changed the subject, asking whether I still see Lizette, and how she always liked Lizette and saw in her an ideal woman, but that Lizette had disappointed her. Lizette would like to live a very classy life, but in essence she is a proletarian, from the family of a locksmith, and she never will have class.

I started showing up with Geraldine in public. She was a good person to be seen with. She knew how to converse pleasantly. She never said no to anything.

Gradually I found out that the fabrics were obtained for her by a Miss Jeanne Fullbridge of the British embassy.

"You know how it is, mama has contacts, through the people who used to be at British Airways."

I deliberately asked no questions about her mama's contacts.

Why put myself in danger?

But at the Medical Students' Ball, I ran into that voluble lady, and was obliged by circumstances to have a dance with her. She carried on her old familiar talk about communists and the absurdity of communism.

"Are you still in heavy engineering, Madame?" I asked.

"Yes, I am," she replied with a laugh. "Isn't that something? So much for their hiring policy!" She was still laughing. "First they spend a year investigating me on account of British Airways, and then they place me in a research lab for heavy engineering! I have access to all the statistics, all the plans—"

"Is that a fact?" I said quickly.

"I know it's incredible," she said, strolling around with me in fox-trot rhythm.

I didn't get it either.

But I intentionally didn't ask any questions.

"And how is your dear mother, Madame?" I preferred asking after the grandmother.

I would meet with Geraldine at noontime in the Koruna automat, where I went for the rum pudding and Geraldine for coffee with whipped cream. That was the sole gastronomical peccadillo she allowed herself. She chattered merrily about her new dress and pumps, about people from the factory, about how people there do nothing but their own outside work, and how there isn't a single fink among them, and once when they tried to place a fink there, the personnel man didn't approve it.

"The personnel man is with the Communists, but he's a real sweetheart," said Geraldine.

In the meantime, the situation for jazz was improving, and Zetka was rehearsing a jazz revue which was aimed, under the pretext of the scientific-historical presentation of the development of the music of the black people of America, at serving the hungry fans of Prague a full portion of the wildest syncopated cocktail that we were capable of mixing.

We utilized all the tricks, which were still necessary, to bring the whole thing to the stage. Including the scholarly discourse of Dr. L. P. Lunda, who—to his own amusement and that of other initiates—deduced the origin of pentatonics from class conflicts in the kingdom of Benin. And including Robert Bulwer, a defector of American origin who was obliged to seek asylum in Czechoslovakia for political reasons, because he didn't want to go in the army. We labeled him a noble successor to Bunk Johnson, and printed his name in big letters on the posters, concealing the proclamation he had made to the Czechoslovak Press Agency in small print inside the program.

On the eve of the concert, Geraldine visited me in my flat.

"What does one wear to the concert? A long evening gown?" she asked. "Or a cocktail dress? Or is an afternoon dress enough?"

"Geraldine, you can come, say, in a bathing suit, you're entitled," I said gallantly, the way she loved it.

"No, seriously," she said, "I'm coming with Jeanne. So

I've got to know." Her black eyes were glowing with enthusiasm, and mingling in the stuffy air of my studio flat, with the smell of the pork roast my landlady Mrs. Ledvinova was making in her kitchen next door, there was a breath of society, Britain and the West.

So I advised her to wear a cocktail dress.

Among the jazz audience that arrived in all the colors of the rainbow, fighting for tickets in front of the theater, she looked like a royal princess.

The dudes swarmed around her like ants around a drop of honey.

For two hours, we blew Dixieland and bebop. The applause that exploded after every number was nearly atomic. Foot stamping, whistling, screaming and yelling the like of which the hall had never experienced before.

After the concert, Geraldine introduced me to Miss Jeanne Fullbridge.

As soon as I set eyes on her, I made my farewells and vanished.

I wasn't interested in a closer acquaintance.

It's like I say, why put yourself in unnecessary danger?

And right I was.

The next morning the phone rang. Lizette. "Did you know they picked up Geraldine and her mother?"

"Come on!"

"No, really, read it in the morning paper."

I rushed down to the newsstand. Miss Jeanne Fullbridge had been expelled by the Government of the Republic on twenty-four hours' notice. With the aid of former employees of the British Airways Company, she had been carrying on industrial espionage, taking advantage of her diplomatic immunity.

In connection with her case, several arrests had been made.

I went over to Lizette's. So far she didn't know any more details. But within the next few days, a lot of things came out. They had also arrested the boy Paul, the one in the conical coat, and turned him loose in about a week. They picked up Professor Vašek of the Faculty of Electronics, and didn't turn him loose. A bunch of people fell into it, from society and elsewhere.

"Idiots," Lizette described them. "They used to hang around there out of snobbism, all excited because Geraldine's old lady was British. Serves them right."

"British from Soho."

"We're not all in English Studies like you," Lizette snapped.

"And why did they do it?" I asked Lizette.

"I don't know," she said. "Geraldine's old lady was a fool, and so was Geraldine."

I expected them to pick me up too, but nothing happened.

"Tell me, Lizette, do you think that Geraldine did spying?" I asked after a time.

"She was dumb enough to," said Lizette. "And her mama was too. She could have figured that they'd come after her. Heavy engineering indeed!"

"That's a fact," I said. "But for crying out loud, what could Geraldine have spied on?"

"Heaven knows," said Lizette. "That woman from the embassy turned her head with nylon and made an errand girl out of her. And now she ups and claims diplomatic immunity and leaves Geraldine to take the rap."

"What else could she do?" I said.

"You think she'd do something if she could?" said Lizette.

"You're right," I said. "Geraldine served her purpose, and now she's expendable."

And then, a week after her twentieth birthday, they gave Geraldine five years.

Her mama got twenty-five.

That didn't bother me too much.

But I did feel sorry for Geraldine.

The Well-Screened Lizette

All animals are equal,
but some are more equal than others.

George Orwell

When they sacked me, they didn't sack Lizette. She got a clean bill of health, even though she had never taken a single exam in six semesters at the university. She hadn't even taken a colloquium. They sacked me, although I had passed five semesters including all necessary exams. But I was an element suspected of sympathies for the West, because everyone knew I played in Zetka's swing band. And also, like a bloody fool, I showed up at the political screening session in colored socks. Fendrych, the cross-eyed Political Inspector with buck teeth, stared at them throughout the session, and every time he asked me an important question—such as "Are you descended from the working class, colleague?" or "Do you believe in God, colleague?"—his eyes threaded the answer out of my socks, as if he was deeply offended by these symbols of bourgeois decadence.

Needless to say, I didn't pass. This same Fendrych passed Lizette, who was under no suspicion of harboring questionable sympathies, and quite rightly so. There was only one thing in the whole world for which Lizette had strong sympathies: Lizette herself.

Obviously, I wasn't present at her evaluation, but I can imagine the scene quite easily: Fendrych stared, but not at socks or anything of the sort. No, I am sure that Lizette had put on her oldest blouse, which bore the marks of rough embraces and working-class ardor. I have no doubt that she stressed the proletarian occupation of her father as stagehand at the National Theater, though normally she referred to her dad as "being with" the National Theater. They didn't question her about his political opinions, because he was a member of the working class; Lizette was thus saved from the need of lying. If Fendrych was blinking at anything, it was Lizette's majestically swelling bosom, or her knees covered with darned working-class stockings, which Lizette skillfully exposed to view, knowing full well that they were worth a pair of positive political points. And so Fendrych passed that green-eyed snake in the grass.

And why not? He had been panting after her for two years and she never fully rejected him, because she never fully rejected anybody who might possibly be of use to her.

She thus stayed on the faculty. Many people declared that they would never understand to their dying day how this beautiful wide-eyed bit of fluff could ever have passed a course in Old Church Slavonic, not to mention pasting together a doctoral dissertation. And on the surface, it does seem incredible, because to this day Lizette isn't sure whether Masaryk is spelled with an "i" or a "y," but anybody with a drop of sense need only take one good gander at Lizette for everything to become crystal clear.

By now, at thirty, Lizette is still a knockout. In America she'd be photographed in Technicolor, posing for Maidenform lingerie.

Looks, plus a cunning as immense as her abysmal ignorance of elementary grammar, minus any consideration for others, minus the slightest trace of altruism, plus exemplary single-mindedness when it comes to her own person.

Take that business with Old Church Slavonic: Lizette showed up for examination at a time when Professor Marek did not expect her and, as she had ascertained in advance, he was alone in his office. With lowered eyelids she confessed that she didn't know a single word of OCS but that she desperately needed a certificate of proficiency in order to pass her political evaluation. Professor Marek intended to get furious, but then he looked at Lizette's bra, then higher into her green eyes. There, he drowned.

And he wrote out a certificate for her.

It cost her a few trips to Hřebenka, where Professor Marek lived with his wife and three children. During those trips she had to listen to his life story. During the last journey he confessed to her that he, too, was bored to tears by Old Church Slavonic, and he offered her safe passage in all exams up to the doctorate, in return for occasional sexual favors. But Lizette was sparing with this kind of merchandise, and since she no longer needed to worry about OCS, she went into reverse and backed out of the garage.

In similarly debonair fashion she conquered literature, Russian, Marxism, everything.

I happen to know, because Lizette had a soft spot for me in her heart, which mellowed to the tones of a tenor sax. That may seem like a violation of natural law, for a stone is a stone; I guess Lizette's heart was simply a special kind of stone. It happened when we played in Vlachovka. Her heart started beating in sync with my solos and after the concert I got to know her well, that green-eyed snake in the grass. Yes, she belonged among a special group of beautiful women, a group that's now dying out; Prague is becoming integrated. Lizette left in time, she slithered out of Prague all the way to Rio de Janeiro, God help her. But even if she were to slither all the way to the moon, in her heart she'd remain a snake in the grass.

As far as the doctorate goes—well, that was a bit more complicated. After carefully surveying the situation she chose psychology as her field of specialization, because she correctly pegged Professor Zajc as the most approachable of her teachers, from a strictly human point of view. She also set her sights on a certain classical philologist, a scholarly young man whose knowledge in the field of Women's Studies was strictly theoretical. Lizette provided him with his first opportunity for practical, preliminary research. Her dissertation was finished within a quarter of a year and it was such an outstanding and inspired piece of work that they asked Lizette to add a historical introduction and submit it as part of her application for tenure. Lizette contented herself with the doctorate.

She had other plans.

That classical philologist never got his own doctorate. After Lizette had thrown him overboard, he took to drinking and behaving in a scandalous manner, and in the end they fired him as an incorrigible bourgeois. He now works in a bar in Ostrava.

While I was fulfilling my military obligations, Lizette's career progressed, though rather modestly at first. She got a job teaching Marxism at a Smíchov high school. Most of her fellow graduates had to become math teachers in the provinces, but Lizette made the timely acquaintance of someone influential in the Ministry of Education, whose name I forget.

By the time I got out of service, she had become program director in the Center for Folk Art. She'd appear in the Alfa Cafe bedecked with gold and precious stones, reminiscent of Geraldine's halcyon days, except that Lizette didn't have to reach into anyone's secret drawers. She had met someone high up in the Ministry of Finance, so that her family was well prepared for the fiscal reform.

As one might expect, Lizette's goings-on did not endear her to everyone, and there were growing numbers of fellows who hated her and voiced nasty insinuations about her whenever they could, but as soon as they found themselves vis-à-vis Lizette and vis-à-vis her bosom, they were bewitched once more into silent adoration.

Communists, noncommunists, Jews.

Fraternal equality.

Even Jan Vrchcoláb, the promising poet from the Youth Movement, fell for her. Lizette's bra blinded him to such an extent that he began to confide to her his ideological dreams and doubts. She told them to me. She had a liking for me, the snake in the grass, though she wasn't too generous with her sexual presents and though in the end she sent me packing, too.

Whenever Vrchcoláb was about to write something for *Youth Front* magazine, he first consulted Lizette. She gave him her advice. And because Lizette, like a true woman, shifted her moods and opinions with astonishing aplomb, Jan Vrchcoláb's opinions changed accordingly, often making a complete about-face. *Youth Front* readers ate it up. Thus, via Vrchcoláb, Lizette exerted a profound influence on the Youth Movement.

Of course, this was a secret.

Actually, no matter what ideas Lizette came up with, at bottom they all focused on one thing: Lizette herself. In that regard, she was remarkably consistent and loyal.

She kept changing Vrchcoláb's views just out of boredom, for the sake of fun. Many people started to scratch their heads, trying to puzzle out Vrchcoláb's philosophy. In vain.

Whenever she put some especially amusing notion into his head, we'd meet at the Alfa and enjoy the joke together. And we would collaborate on new nonsense to pump into him. He was in the habit of beating his gums in public about every new cultural or political event, and he was unaware that he'd become a dummy for a pair of ventriloquists.

His remarks, regularly reprinted in *Youth Front,* stimulated polemics and weighty discussions. Various socialist-realist theoreticians analyzed and expounded Lizette's bebop profundities, giving rise to a virtual new literary movement. Some articles were published in the Soviet Union, from there they were taken over by *L'Humanité,* then they appeared in *The Masses & Mainstream.* In this way, Lizette's influence extended across the Atlantic Ocean.

We developed an appetite for this kind of amusement, and began to target various prominent persons: via Vrchcoláb, we accused them of cosmopolitanism, bourgeois nationalism, Zionism, Mendel-Morganism, formalism, and kowtowing to Western culture. We branded them as henchmen of Slánský or Tito, lackeys of naturalism, Freudianism, idealism, spiritualism, opportunism, revisionism, surrealism; we excoriated them for their fluency in English. Via Vrchcoláb, we carried on our campaign in private, at meetings, in the course of political evaluation sessions, and to some extent in the press.

Naturally, Vrchcoláb suffered the consequences. He is still suffering.

In the end, he managed to help place Lizette on the preparatory committee for the Sofia exposition, and thereby his usefulness for Lizette came to an involuntary yet definite end. Lizette's contribution to the preparatory committee proved predictably disastrous. But before she bowed out, she fulfilled one requirement set by the committee's director, Comrade Borecký: he asked the women employed by the organization to order, at state expense, three dresses from the fashionable Rosenbaum couturier, in order to represent our country abroad in a proper manner.

Lizette fulfilled this directive so ardently that she ordered not three, but six dresses from Rosenbaum's.

She screwed up whatever she touched, but the director became fond of her all the same. He called her "our Lizzy," even in front of the press. As a result, one young woman reporter, who had been ass-kissing Borecký in the hope that he would get her a job at the ministry, was encouraged to shoot an interview with Lizette for the upcoming exposition, presenting her as a typical socialist woman of our day.

Well, the reporter made quite a boo-boo, but nobody knew it at the time.

Before leaving for Sofia, there came a directive from above that the unduly overgrown staff was to be cut by a third. They threw out Maršíkova, who had been putting in two hours a day extra without pay. They threw out Béhmová, who had organized all the pavilions dealing with industrial machinery, light as well as heavy. They even threw out Tatyana Letnic-Sommernitz, who was political officer and supervisor of the Workers' Brigade.

History repeated itself once more: Lizette went to

Sofia. She took along all six Rosenbaum creations, in addition to various items to trade and exchange. The cases of
Riša's bass fiddle and my tenor sax were filled to overflow-
ing.

You see, we went along, too. Zetka's Swing Orchestra.
That was the only thing that Lizette managed to do right.
When it came to gags and practical jokes, you could always
count on Lizette.

And so we introduced Sofia to the folk music of the
oppressed American blacks. We ourselves weren't oppressed in any way, although we were given strict instructions by the Ministry of Culture. We shot the works. Night
after night, hundreds of male and female Sofians stomped
and swayed on the floor, to the sounds of Benny Good-
man. Lizette was among them, accompanied by various
swains and later by a tall, blond man from their Ministry of
Culture.

He, too, started calling her Lizcttc. Her name was actually Lidmila, but she had all sorts of nicknames: Lída,
Liduše, Líza. That handsome Bulgarian called her Lizette,
and it stuck.

After a few days they took off for a seaside resort. Of
course, that was against regulations, the exposition was under strict discipline, but did that matter to Lizette? What a
naive idea.

She joined us in Budapest, on our return trip, and she
was escorted by a new admirer. He looked like an under-

cover policeman. The devil knows what he was, but with Lizette anything was possible.

She had brought back with her a TV set, a silver fox cape, a Persian rug, a calculator, two cameras, a gold watch and some twenty decagrams of gold jewelry. Also, six meters of Chinese silk with a pagoda design, but she sold it because Prague was overstocked with that particular item.

And she got away with it. The other women, each of whom was returning with one nylon nightshirt and two liters of maraschino, gnashed their teeth in fury. They hated her. Pokorná actually denounced her, but the report dissolved somewhere in the secret files of the Ministry of the Interior.

In Sofia, before she turned her back on the exposition and vamoosed with her blond companion, Lizette managed to bewitch the deputy director, Řericha, an extremely influential figure in education. He blazed up like an Olympic flame.

He arranged a public appearance for her. In the name of Czech women, she addressed the children of Bulgaria on the occasion of their new school year, and her speech was carried by all the Bulgarian media.

Back in Czechoslovakia, it was cited in the press.

She and I had composed the speech one early morning in the exposition dance hall, under the influence of heady Bulgarian wine.

Fortunately, nobody pays any attention to such addresses, and they are promptly forgotten.

Lizette, however, was not forgotten. Hardly had she returned to Prague and put in a voucher for an additional three thousand crowns in expenses than Deputy Director Řeřicha made her assistant editor of the State Pedagogic Publishing House. The candidate slated for that position, an experienced pedagogue, was suddenly discovered to be a dry intellectual of bourgeois origin, with insufficient Marxist erudition.

In comparison with Lizette's proletarian background, this was a serious shortcoming.

And because Lizette didn't have to start from the bottom, her deficiencies in elementary grammar never came to light.

You have to hand it to Lizette: she never forgot old friends. Trusted translators, employed for years by the publishing house, were dropped and translation assignments were distributed to Lizette's buddies instead. I benefited, too. With the help of a pocket dictionary, I translated from the Russian some poems of Mao Tse-tung, as well as a handbook of criminal law.

Lizette never learned of the disastrous consequences.

At a writers' congress, Lizette met a man from the Foreign Ministry. A month later she was named cultural attaché in Rio de Janeiro, in place of a fellow named Hrubeš who had been studying Portuguese for five years in expectation of the assignment.

I know, it sounds unbelievable, the mind rebels against it, and yet it's a fact.

There are many mysteries twixt heaven and earth.

Political evaluation, class origin, socialist zeal, merit, are one thing; generous bosom, shapely behind, green eyes are another.

Like time and eternity.

I don't know how you may feel about it, but I would never dare weigh one against the other.

Anyway, that snake in the grass Lizette who left so many in the lurch—including me—is in Rio, sitting pretty as cultural attaché.

I expect that one day she'll become the first woman president of this country.

And then at last we'll have real socialism.

Krpata's Blues

Got 'em blues, am' damn,
Mean to cry, O Lord!

They locked up Krpata.

I wasn't surprised; in fact, I was glad. In my opinion, it saved his life. For a while, at least.

During the four years that Krpata piped on the clarinet with us, his performance of the blues improved remarkably. When we took him on, Krpata had a decent technique, but a hard, steely, even tone—no talent, it seemed, for making the instrument sing—but he excelled at jokes and pranks: for instance, maybe we're playing some big band Count Basie, and I switch to tenor sax and sidle up to the microphone since it's my turn to show off with a solo, but when I blow into the sax I get this horrible mooing sound. Of course, the "sharp boys" in the front rows stiffen, the "sidecar girls" drop their preparations for an extra bumpy fox-trot on the dance floor and stare at me in amazement, and I blush and sweat and conjure up frightful noises—Zetka gets up from the piano—I reach into the bell of the sax and pull out a crumpled pair of pink nylon panties, monogrammed, with lace. The gag sends the sharp boys over the edge, the bobby-soxers shriek enthusiastically, salvo after salvo of applause. I have to grin and bow.

That was the kind of prank Krpata used to pull.

Time-honored, but always effective.

And then he got married and the pranks started to dry up. And as they dried up, his clarinet began to weep

and moan, his tone softened, it took shape, it got beauti-
fully and lyrically rougher; during Dixieland jazz he would
slowly steal the cornet's lead, until finally he took it so far
that nobody danced during Dixie jazz; they listened close,
shed tears, watched Krpata with his caved-in chest and tu-
bercular face, with his half-closed eyes and that miracu-
lous, sweet, bluesy woodwind, watched him play the blues.

What blues!

Really the blues.

Not infrequently, some sharp boy well on his way to
getting drunk would burst into tears.

And now they've put him away for attempting to bribe
administrators of the people's government and for libel of
a police officer; they took away his clarinet and gave him a
shovel.

That's how they saved his life, for a while anyway, because to keep playing the way he was playing was no longer
an option. By now it would have gone beyond the limits of
bearable. Best-case scenario, it would have driven him
crazy, the way marijuana did to Leon Rappolo.

Krpata's story is as follows:

Out of love, he married a girl named Květuše
Procházková, and out of light-headedness, he forgot to
take care of the chief and fundamental thing, the most important thing in every love and every marriage: the apartment.

At this point, boredom is probably descending on you

with the heavy pall of apartment anecdotes from the state humor magazine *Dikobraz*.

But this time it isn't an anecdote, but as it were, the true-life story of the private tragedy and artistic growth of Ladislav Krpata, blues clarinetist. Květuše was just a regular girl, a little peroxide, a little makeup, one day with her hair bobbed, the next day plastered down Roman style, another day plain Jane, long and straight—just like most girls, really, with the usual desires for a nylon nightgown and a hand-knit shepherd's sweater from Italy for six hundred crowns.

He was the only one who could see what was special about her; I couldn't see it.

But that's the way it always is, isn't it.

Up until he hung her around his neck, he lodged in Žižkov with a lady named Rosalie Ledvinová, who rented the room exclusively to single gentlemen, because girls, she said, would always be cooking something and washing and drying, which makes a mess, and she didn't want any of that in the apartment.

With good reason. Aside from the three-by-four-meter room to let, she only had a kitchen, slightly smaller—unless you count the so-called antechamber. Relatively speaking, though, this widow was well-off, with a full four hundred in pension. Which, with the two-fifty she got from Krpata, came to a clean six hundred fifty.

Pretty good, hunh?

Of course, there are widows who do better, because they're resourceful widows. For instance, our drummer lives with one who instead of rooms has a boardinghouse. She has a kind of bungalow. It's listed as a family home; downstairs there's her apartment, on the second floor five cubicles, and in the attic another two. Seven altogether, with ten lodgers, all told. Three at two-fifty, in singles; eight at two-zero-zero (these are doubled up in cubicles); and one—how should I put it—one "honeymoon suite," the most expensive, actually: it costs fifty to a hundred crowns per visit. So that in total she gets twenty-one hundred a month out of the place, not counting the honeymoon suite.

You don't believe me? I can give you the address, if you're interested. There's no vacancy right now, although of course that one "suite" is always available.

But I've gotten sidetracked; this isn't what we're talking about here.

Krpata was living at the widow Ledvinová's at the time, and since he was naive and trusting, he followed her advice. Her advice was that he should never have anything to do with the housing department. For this reason, he lived in her house without a sublettor's license—that is, in his simplicity he didn't even know about the existence of this kind of document—he merely registered with the police and simply: lived there. The widow, just so you don't think ill of her, was not being crafty, not at all, but she was afraid of the housing department. Old women are always timid; they're afraid of vampires and murderers, and this one was afraid they would take her little apartment away from her and move her out to the border regions.

Well, now, the trouble was that Květuše Procházková was a proletarian daughter from Karlín and she lived with her parents in a kind of extra romantic apartment with a porch that faced a courtyard, like in Neruda's stories: you went from the porch into the main room, through the main room into the kitchen, and there the apartment ended. The apartment had another rare advantage: it was on the opposite end of the porch from the toilet, so you couldn't smell the septic tank, just laundry and rotten cabbage.

When the young couple committed their imprudence, they imagined that Květuše could move into Krpata's lodgings, and then when the widow Ledvinová kicked the bucket, they would grab the apartment.

Naturally, this was brutal and inhumane calculation on their part.

So in the end maybe they got what they deserved.

And Krpata should stew.

Only, it didn't work; they ran into the widow. She shrieked, the way widows shriek, that she had rented the apartment to a single gentleman, and if the single gentleman got married, he should look for an apartment elsewhere. She would not let another woman into her apartment; in her apartment, she said, one woman was enough.

To be honest, she was right.

Well, there was nothing to be done; they couldn't force the widow. For the first time, Krpata did a little research into the law on apartments; it astounded him that he hadn't read it sooner, but he figured out this much pretty quick: that a lodger has uncommonly few rights. Definitely not the right to move his wife in.

They decided therefore that while they were looking for an apartment they would live apart, she with her parents in Karlín and he at the widow Ledvinová's in Žižkov, which in the end wasn't so bad, because they weren't far from each other.

As for connubial bliss, they visited each other regularly. On Sunday afternoons Krpata went to Květuše's while her parents were at the soccer match, and on Wednesday afternoons Květuše came to Krpata's, because every Wednesday afternoon the widow Ledvinová went out for coffee. Of course, on Sunday they couldn't start before Květuše's parents went off to the soccer match, which took place at 2:30, and they had to be through by 6:30, when her parents returned from soccer, their mood altered according to the final score. On Wednesday it was even more meager, since they couldn't start until after 6:00, when Květuše flew in from the store, and they had to finish by 7:45, the latest Krpata could wait to go to work.

They filed an application for an apartment. They were placed in a category, assigned a number of points—I don't understand the system, because I don't care to; why should I care, when it doesn't have anything to do with me? I'm not longing for marriage and I have a place on Rajský Hill in a suburban home that belongs to a composer, with a view of Prague, a yard, a bathroom, and a telephone available for me to use. How did I get this, if I used to live like Krpata? Well now, that's a secret, sweethearts, and understandably so.

They gave Krpata points because he was married, because he lived in a sublet apart from his wife, because it was a house more than fifty years old, because there was no bath in his father-in-law's house, because the kitchen window faced north—but this was actually somewhat neutralized by the door to the main room, which faced south—because the apartment was damp, because it did not contain the required X square meters per person, because it had no gas, because it was a long way from the trolley car stop, because Květuše's father was an incurable bed wetter, etc. etc.

This, in short, was how they gave out points.

As time went by, the points started to increase. In the fall, water seeped into the apartment from the roof—there were quite a few points for that. Under the flooring in the kitchen they discovered mildew. More points. For the bedbugs in the main room, however, they refused to award any points, and merely recommended that they buy something to get rid of them, but on the other hand they did grant them something for the basement, which flooded when a spring of sulfur water suddenly gushed forth; later, however, the water turned out to be the fluid content of a burst sewage line, so they took the points back again. Krpata began to remind me of a stockbroker; he went to the housing department regularly, notebook in hand, adding up points.

He lacked one important thing. A child. They gave lots of points for that.

So they produced one.

And fortune smiled on them. When the child was born, the widow Ledvinová abruptly died.

She ate some spoiled salami that she had squirreled away ages ago and got meat poisoning.

But.

It was established that Krpata had no sublettor's license.

It was further established that he was married.

Consequently in the long run he had somewhere to live.

Consequently they flushed him out of the apartment, on the heels of the widow Ledvinová.

This, together with the child, drastically increased the number of points.

Well, except you would have to know Krpata, and his domestic jewel Květuše too. He's a dimwit. When they threw him out, he couldn't manage a word of protest. On the contrary. In his perverse, point-filled brain he saw it as a great blessing, and immediately and joyously rushed to the housing department so they could credit him with the points right away.

Well, why not? They credited him with the points.

And he moved into Květuše's parents' place. They weren't too happy about this. Hard to expect them to be happy about it, although as parents perhaps they were supposed to be.

But I have to describe this married couple a little. Květuše's mama was a Mother-In-Law with a big M, big I, and big L. She had a habit of standing with her hands on her hips; she had hips like that fertility goddess they unearthed in Věstonice and a facial expression like a French bulldog's. Need I say more.

She worked in the town market hall in Královské Vinohrady.

And Daddy paved streets for a living.

That's right. What d'you think, under socialism they no longer needed people to pave the streets?

Maybe now you'll understand that the day Krpata moved in with his wife's family, he vigorously stepped up his point-related efforts.

And his clarinet also began to acquire a cantilena tone and at the same time a rough timbre; it got more and more bluesy.

But somehow it seemed that they still didn't have

enough of those points. They were already near the top of the chart, in maybe third or fourth place after a consumptive with two children and a fertile family without tuberculosis but with triplets and a second set on the way.

They couldn't budge from this position. Somehow, someone far behind them would always gain points suddenly and skip over not only them but also the family with potential sextuplets and the one with tuberculosis.

That "somehow" isn't as mysterious as it sounds.

But in this world you need a little smarts.

And that's what Krpata didn't have.

He played bluesier and bluesier blues, until finally, at long last, the light dawned and he realized he wasn't going to get very far with those points, and he would have to start cheating.

And once again he got lucky.

But once again he went about it in the wrong way.

He was all lit up with hope when he played *Tiger Rag* that night. He had the whole Bulvárka on its feet.

The plan involved a cousin who was supposed to be transferred from Prague to the border regions, where an apartment in a suburban home had been placed at his disposal. In Prague this cousin lived with his wife in a studio in a first-class modern apartment building with a lava facade in Pankrác, which must have seemed like paradise to Krpata.

This is what they dreamed up: they would take Krpata

and Květuše on as lodgers, then they would move out, and Krpata would take advantage of a certain paragraph and section of the law, according to which, if the owner of an apartment moves out, the sublettor has priority to it if he is married and has children.

With great ceremony, Krpata and Květuše and their son canceled their registration with the Karlin police and registered with the police in Pankrác.

They then went to request a sublettor's license. They were told there wouldn't be any problem.

The law, however, remembers everything.

They saw through the ruse, declared it to be an attempt at housing fraud, and told them to get lost.

For that matter, it's against the law for sublettors to move into a studio, especially if it's occupied by a husband and wife.

Still, they could be glad they didn't get in any serious trouble for it.

So they canceled their registration in Pankrác and re-registered in Karlín. And then nothing special happened to them.

Well, all right. Krpata went at the problem from another angle. He decided to build a do-it-yourself family home on Rajský Hill out of synthetic building materials. As a result he toiled through the whole prom season like a horse; he would make the rounds of maybe three proms a night; in the morning he helped out at the radio; in the afternoon he would play funerals with a brass band; in the evening blues at the Bulvárka, and after midnight in some night club.

In a short time he had saved up the sum needed to purchase the synthetic building materials and the plot of land, and he requested a construction permit.

Again, of course, he did everything straightforward and aboveboard. It never occurred to him that even with synthetic building materials one should proceed somewhat differently.

He didn't look for protection, intervention, nothing.

He simply filed a request.

And on top of that he sent it by mail.

Simply put—Krpata.

As you can imagine, his application was processed smoothly. That is, negatively.

I thought he was going to have a stroke. He came to Barrandov one evening—it was already spring, the prom season was over, and we were playing outside on the terraces—his whole body was trembling and he looked like a nervous wreck. I took pity on him. He was already just a shadow of the old Krpata, of the one who stuffed ladies' nylon panties down the bell of my saxophone. I sat down next to him and got the whole story out of him. Afterward, when we played *Heartbreak Blues,* five trashed sharp boys and one quite sober lady burst into tears.

Then I took him in hand. Simply put—I'm not going

to describe it to you in detail—look, here and there, we—pretty soon, things were progressing very nicely.

But during the waiting period, he and his wife came to visit me at Rajský Hill on a Monday night we had free.

We sat on the terrace; it was a warm evening, almost summer; against the light blue sky of Hradčany, the moon looked like a drop of honey someone was shining a flashlight behind; red light fell on the sunflowers on Petrin Hill; below us, the Vltava was full of dinghies and rowboats; trees rustled in the gardens along the hillside; reflections of green water in pools glanced through the fences of suburban homes—it was romantic, like a bad movie.

"Who lives here?" Krpata asked, his voice trembling with envy.

"You mean in this house?" I said. "Oh, some fellow named Bernát, a composer."

"Just him—in this whole house?" Krpata said.

"Yeah," I said. "I'm in this room, and the rest is his."

"And how many rooms does he have?"

"Three," I said. "He has a workroom, since as a composer he has a right to that by virtue of his occupation, then a bedroom, and then another room, since after all it's his house. And he's a composer."

"I don't know him," Krpata interrupted me.

"Your loss," I said. "It's not his fault you're just a jazz barbarian. He composes cantatas and songs for the workers' movement."

Krpata fell silent and surveyed the fantastic, formalist, purely cosmopolitan houses all around.

He gulped. Then in a loud voice he shouted: "Shit!"

Květuše rebuked him, primly.

"Calm down and breathe deeply," I said. "Don't yell at me here, or I'll have a real mess on my hands and that'll be it for your family home made out of synthetic building materials."

But Krpata again shouted: "Fuck me!" until it reverberated around the spire of the new boathouse down by the river.

"You moron," I said. "What are you yelping about? Be happy you're about to get a cozy home in the pipeline, a home made out of synthetic building materials and in the traditional architectural style of the Czech people, and don't trouble yourself with anything more than that, or you'll ef dot dot dot everything up again."

Even I didn't realize how timely my warning was.

But in the meantime there was a lesser mishap. I'd put the fix in with a certain gentleman regarding Krpata's synthetic home for five thousand crowns (the price of the gentleman, not the house), but the guy got thrown in the slammer. Several things blew up in his face; fortunately, ours wasn't one of them.

Krpata was back where he started, but five thousand lighter.

They nailed the gentleman right after the bribe.

When it rains, it pours.

So the little house made out of synthetic building materials melted away.

After this debacle, Krpata understandably began to have the impression that fate was at work here. He began to spend some time contemplating the bottom of his beer glass, which had one tragic consequence: Květuše suddenly found herself with another bun in the oven.

In Bulvárka, alcohol flow rose by twenty percent. In a sober state it wasn't possible to listen to Krpata play blues clarinet. It affected us too, made us let go, made us abandon ourselves to the music.

An American tourist offered us a gig at the Cotton Club.

Dreamland.

And meanwhile Krpata, the idiot, without my knowledge, without telling anyone, started up on his own.

This time, as it later became clear, he was through with the straight and narrow, with application forms and the awarding of points; he was going to cheat.

Naively, the same way he'd grubbed for points and mailed in applications.

He drank like a fish, his cheeks darkened to an unhealthy shade of red, and his thin, bony fingers scattered over the clarinet like over calculator keys.

One night the cop sent to monitor Bulvárka to ensure no lewd dances were danced broke into sobs.

And then they nailed Krpata.

The idiot went to the housing authority right after some fuckup they had there, when they were all running scared and extra cautious, and he stuffed five thousand into the desk officer's pocket practically in broad daylight.

Naturally the guy exposed him on the spot.

He scored a few points as an incorruptible bureaucrat.

And they nailed Krpata.

When they took him away, he resisted arrest and made statements and even, they say, physically assaulted the police officer.

Now he's cooling his heels—actually, working like a dog—and as I say, maybe it's saved his life, for a little while.

Because the way he'd been playing the blues was the brink of suicide.

Naturally I don't know what will happen when they let him out.

But that's not my problem either, is it?

The Bebop of Richard Kambala

You probably don't know where Bop comes from—
Every time a cop hits a Negro with a billy club,
that old club says Bop! Bop!—Bebop!—Bop!

Langston Hughes

This is the story of Richard Kambala, and may it remain his obituary. There won't be any words lost on him anyway, and they don't even put a notice in *Musical Review* when a jazz musician dies.

Especially when he kills himself.

Because it's like a confirmation of the formula that starts with cosmopolitan music, proceeds through hepcats, and winds up with existentialism and suicide.

For that matter, maybe the formula is true. I don't claim it isn't.

But why?

That *why* is at the beginning of all things, and at the end of them. And as for what's in between—

Well, some people know how to live even between those two *whys*, and don't give a damn if anyone answers them or not. But Kambala probably wasn't one of those people.

And so this is his obituary.

I don't know when he was born, but it was in Prague, and his father was in import-export. And it was definitely a wrong time to be born, for the son of a man who was in import-export.

That was also why they kept him out of high school. Naturally. Because what kind of fine feathered fellows would the cadre selection guys be, in the words of Charles Davida, if once in a while they didn't grab a millionaire's boy by the scruff of his neck when he was trying to squeeze through to a higher education, or if they didn't see to it now and then that some ex-prisoner couldn't get a job anywhere, except maybe as the most manual of laborers.

In this case, they were true to form and kept Kambala out, and instead they forced his best friend Josef Vořech to go—the perfect model of a country yokel who just happened to live in Prague, where his dad was overseer at the state farm in Jinonice. Josef Vořech! A red-headed kid whose ears stuck out like signal flags, who had loved cows and hay and the smell of alfalfa ever since he was little and who always wanted to go live in the country up near the border as soon as he finished grade ten. They forced him to go to high school, and he struggled to get through it like a camel through the eye of a needle, and then, when he wanted at least to go study agriculture—

Ah well, now he's still busting his buns at the College of Engineering, and Saturdays he sits at the Alfa Cafe, staring at us with watery eyes and crying. He's been crying ever since Kambala did it. He was his best friend.

Anyway, they forced Vořech in even though he had bad grades, because his father was a rural proletarian. They kept Kambala out because his grades were too good and he was the son of a capitalist and who knows, something might become of him and he might somehow harm the people's democratic regime.

So Vořech attended high school and Kambala was an

apprentice at the Ringhoffer plant. Both of them were peeved.

Vořech floundered in high school like a fish out of water, occasionally boosted by some scared comrade professor, while Kambala did his best at the Ringhoffer plant. He crammed, he slaved, he was active in the Czechoslovak Union of Youth, he played guitar in the musical ensemble, he bellowed progressive songs and he wore a blue shirt to work.

He had no other choice, did he, wanting what he wanted. And finally he accomplished it. They accepted him at the vocational high school.

He was seventeen already. But they accepted him. He was recommended by his plant, so they accepted him.

When he made friends with us, he had been there a year. A strange case—he couldn't afford a trumpet, but he scrounged up an old fluegelhorn someplace, and that's what he played. We promoted him as a star attraction, hot fluegelhorn, world sensation, and he performed with us twice a week at the Boulevard Cafe.

Under a pseudonym, of course.

Meanwhile—and it was really touching—he still hung around with Vořech, the yokel from Jinonice. The cadre selection guys hadn't broken up their friendship. As a matter of fact, the two of them formed a fluegelhorn and vocal duo, which wailed and played at dances Sunday after Sunday in the villages around Prague.

I went to hear them once. You simply wouldn't believe that this could exist a few kilometers from the Boulevard Cafe and from Wenceslas Square. It was a tiny village in the Dobříš district, a tavern with a dingy dance hall, with a hand-lettered sign by the door which read: HOLIDAY DANCE, MUSIC BY MR. URAL'S BAND, 5 CROWNS A TICKET. And inside, the place was crowded with crackers like Vořech, girls with shoulders straight out of a fashion magazine imported from Moscow, smoke and liquor fumes, and on the old-fashioned platform with a carved railing sat Vořech and Kambala, each of them blowing his horn, accompanied by some old geezers on clarinet, fiddle, accordion, bass, and drums.

And every so often they would sing. God, it was enough to make you cry, even with all those stupidities, to see Kambala standing there, pale and dandy, with his hair in a d.a., and his aristocratic countenance, standing in front of the band with Vořech, arms around each other's shoulders, singing in that uniquely polka manner where nobody cares about details like having the same number of syllables as notes in their melodies. Singing, head to head, immobile except for their mouths opening and closing, Vořech's pancake ears glowing like a neon sign, sincere tears flowing from his blue eyes to his rosy cheeks. The two of them singing, Kambala carrying the melody in his tenor voice, deformed by the polka style, and above him Vořech, big and blustery—he could have swallowed Kambala after lunch—singing harmony in his eunuch's falsetto, slicing the syllables for all they're worth:

Where is that love
weshared . . . soften . . . derlee?

So while Kambala attended vocational high school, Vořech studied at high school until finally, with all the scared professors and informed commission chairmen, he was pushed through the sieve of matriculation exams. And then, by the same methods, they shoved him through the entrance exams at the College of Engineering, where he didn't want to go but where they were short of students. Now, if he was going to have to undergo all the unpleasantness connected with studying, Vořech would have preferred, as I have mentioned, to attend the College of Agriculture. But of course, in the end, he had to obey and go where society was supposed to have needed him most. Or so society thought. At least, that's what they said so they didn't have to say that they were simply ordering him to go there.

Naturally, Kambala had no trouble at all getting through vocational high school, it was child's play for him, and after school he studied college textbooks. Because that fool had set his mind on becoming a mechanical engineer.

Anyway—

Meanwhile, his dad, formerly in import-export, was

working in a warehouse in Kbely. Then one day they arrested him.

We never did find out why. There was nothing about it in the newspapers, and Kambala didn't know for sure either. The only one who might have known was the dad himself, or maybe the prosecuting attorney knew—well, what can I tell you, you know how it goes.

That doesn't mean that I think he never did anything. I'm sure he did. Like maybe bad-mouthing current conditions, since he used to be in import-export. Or maybe telling a joke.

Or maybe he was in contact with enemy intelligence or maybe he was appropriating the property of the people.

I don't know.

Anything is possible.

Except that's not the point, where Kambala is concerned. The point was something else.

So Kambala played with us Wednesdays and Saturdays as Lajos Kerdely, Hungarian fluegelhorn player, a sensation in Budapest and the world. As sometimes happens—he was a relatively good-looking fellow—he fell into the trap set for him by Marcella Růžičková, whose name on posters was Cella Rose and who performed at various joints, singing songs like *Ghost Riders in the Sky* and *C'est si bon* and various other hits of the early post-Stalinist era in Prague. In matters of the heart, Kambala was still a rookie, and so he glowed like the filament of a two-hundred-watt bulb.

The principal at the vocational school was a particular dope. For example: he had installed a huge alcohol thermometer with a sign: THERMOMETER OF LOVE FOR JOSEF VISSARIONOVICH STALIN. In the winter, they had to put an electric heater by it.

Enough said.

And then, in the autumn of the year of our Lord 1955, instructions arrived from the Ministry of Education, that in the interest of conscientious attention to the prudent selection of reliable cadres, children of citizens imprisoned for crimes against the state are to be dropped immediately from specialized schools, that is to say, kicked out.

It would be interesting to know what kind of thinking from what kind of brain gives rise to instructions like that. One is forced to recall, willy-nilly, the case of Dr. Bohadlo, that great progressive from Pankrác prison—but you know that story already.

Simply, the dope who was principal of the vocational high school obeyed, as is the wont of dopes, to the minute and to the letter. That is to say he went directly to the classroom of the fourth-year students, where they were just having a lesson in the Czech language, tossed Kambala out of the room bodily with his own two hands and a scowl of class hatred, and accompanied him outside in front of the school building, barely allowing him into the cloakroom to get his coat.

Later on, the Czech professor, a certain Milada Kalinová, a maid who could justly be called old, stood up for Kambala in the teachers' staff room, pointing out his excellent marks, his activity in the Youth Union, and finally something that she considered obvious, blind to the fact that it's not that simple: that children can't help the sins of their parents.

It slipped her mind that they often pay the penalty for them, however.

Well, old maids are frequently naive, there's nothing new about that.

Nor did she get away with it. The comrades in the staff room had for some time been observing her political instability, that is to say, comrade principal had been observing her, and the staff room went along with his observations. She received a strict reprimand.

Later on, I found out that for a similar affair—standing up for some student who had written some vulgar verse about the erstwhile Thermometer of Love—she had been fired.

Apparently, nobody missed her.

Actually, in those days the law about the exacerbation of the class struggle was still considered to be in effect.

But it did Kambala in.

First he fell apart, then he pulled himself together a little and began making a living with his fluegelhorn. Three evenings a week with us, Sundays and Saturday afternoons with Vořech and Mr. Ural's band, Thursdays at jam sessions at Drahňovský's nightclub with a bebop trio consisting of fluegelhorn, bassoon and drums, and the rest of the time, wherever. He made his way any way he could, and he clung to the aforementioned Marcella like flypaper.

He had an inner attachment to her.

Poor guy, he was simply young and inexperienced.

Because it's a commonly known fact that what appeals to women is a man, i.e., a Man, if not a MAN—but someone who hangs on to them, needs them, loves them to distraction, in fact so much that he can't live without them, someone like that merely annoys them.

In short, the same old story.

In Kambala's case it was just like that.

As long as he was Lajos Kerdely, sensation in Budapest and the world, a rather happy and frivolous kid with his hair in a d.a., who would occasionally go silly around Marcella when the situation warranted, but who for the most part let her run after him because his head was full of engineering and music and what they called the Future, Marcella could have doused herself with all the perfume in the world to at least get him to take a whiff of her. But when he melted like butter in someone's pocket, and began to look to her for understanding and something like moral support in life's difficulties, naturally, Cella was not amused, she was not impressed.

For that matter, what is there about that kind of behavior that could and would impress a woman?

Cella Marcella simply gave him the cold shoulder.

As for him, unfortunate fool that he was, after all the blows that his young life had dealt him he, naturally, went ahead and did exactly the wrong thing.

He wept, he begged, etcetera, he pursued her, he pled, sent her presents.

Marcella got together with Tony Bantam, a crooner from the Cafe Vltava.

One night in the men's room at the Cafe Vltava, Bantam took Kambala and turned him upside down with a professional clout, a left to the chin.

And then—

There isn't much more to tell. It was Thursday, and a bunch of us went to Drahňovský's club after work for a jam session. Around midnight, Kambala came limping in with his bebop trio. Without a word, they got up on stage, the fellow with the bassoon moistened his reeds, and then they let go and began to fall.

And fall they did—the way they fell, everyone there was sick to his stomach. And the people that go there for the most part aren't philosophers, but rather select hepcats and their very superficial lady friends. They fell in major seconds and in diminished fifths, down and down, immobile, someone put a blue spotlight on them and the people in the room quit talking, just gaped and listened.

And I'll never forget the way Kambala looked.

He stood tall and straight, his fluegelhorn twisted like

a pretzel by his mouth, and as he toyed with the keys, you couldn't even see him inhale or anything. His face was expressionless. His eyes were on the edge of the bell or wherever. And he played—or God knows just what he was doing. Close by him the obscure little gnome of a guy with whiskers and a bassoon creaked and creaked and grumbled, while behind them De Martini scrunched down, softly rustling his cymbals.

Horrible music.

Existentialism in unwritten notes.

They played something, I couldn't tell what, nobody could tell, not even them, except probably Kambala, they played it for exactly thirty-seven minutes without a break.

Then they split.

The hepcats applauded for ten minutes more, but nobody came back, no encore.

Suddenly I was overcome with an evil premonition, I slipped outside, but Kambala was already gone.

I caught a streetcar and went after him. He lived in a villa in Strešovice, in an attic room that they rented out to him.

When I got there, it was raining. I climbed the fence and there was a light on in his room. Then I saw Kambala by the window in his pyjamas, brushing his teeth.

It seemed dumb to ring the bell and say something to him, besides, what could I say, in fact it began to seem to me that I had acted rashly and foolishly in coming. That I simply, well, have a strong reaction to music, and maybe this time Kambala had succeeded with his thirty-seven-minute uninterrupted bebop in getting Marcella and all the rest of it out of his system.

So I turned on my heel and went home.

Except it wasn't that way at all.

The next evening, Josef Vořech burst into the Boulevard Cafe, his blue eyes reddened and tears streaming down his chin.

"Fellows, Kambala is dead," he says.

I jumped up, because it sliced through my spine like an electric shock.

"What?"

"Yes, guys," says Vořech, pressing a blue farmer's handkerchief to his face. "He did himself in, guys, oh, oh!"

In short, it turned out that when Kambala finished brushing his teeth, he lay down on the bed, stuck a grenade in his mouth and pulled the pin.

If only yesterday I'd—

But what if I had. If they hadn't—

No, thinking about it in the conditional is useless.

And so this, then, is the obituary of Richard Kambala, hot fluegelhorn and bebop virtuoso, sensation in Budapest and the world. May at least his memory remain.

Till Death Do Us Part

So I returned, and considered all the oppressions
that are done under the sun . . .

ECCLESIASTES 4:1

When you play the tenor sax, sooner or later you ask yourself the question.

What's it really for and why and so forth and so on.

Life, that is.

The saxophone is, I'd say, the most revolutionary invention in the history of music. Because it speaks. Almost like a person; better, actually. It doesn't say words. It says essence.

Of course, Jack Teagarden, Kid Ory, etc. can speak on the trombone. And good old Dippermouth on the trumpet. And Billy Butterfield.

But the instrument that really speaks is the saxophone.

And the tenor sax, especially.

You can't sing on it like on the clarinet, or holler like on the trumpet, or roar like the trombone.

But you can speak.

It's the humanistest instrument in the world.

Just listen to it.

So very good sax player sooner or later asks the question, especially because, when you earn your bread in some neon pisshole and instead of looking at the sheet music you look out at the waxed ring where both sexes twitch back and forth, you learn something about life.

Sometimes you learn quite a bit.

And then all of the sudden you're curious, what's it for and why and does it ever pay off.

Of course it's not a question they're handing out answers to.

You're only left with the dim suspicion that it's all the way it is just because—for its own sake, for fun, and for the sake of the joke—and that's no use to a person.

If at least a person knew for sure that one day he would wave his winglets and flutter through the cafes and see what the "sharp boys" and "sidecar girls" he used to know were doing, and how they were, before he ran out of gas.

I.e., died.

But the odds of that are negligible.

Better not to think about it.

And so one prefers to look around and observe people's fates.

Consequently, here they are.

For example, this tall, freckled, bearded man showing off with a gigolo's fox-trot a la 1929. And the black-haired, black-eyed girl with him.

Arnošt Karásek and Paulina Trnková, known as Polly.

She's not much good at polishing the dance floor, she sways back and forth in his arms somewhat as if she had a crick in her neck. He, as I said, is straight out of Cafe Lloyd, 1929. R. A. Dvorský and his Melody Boys.

When you consider what they've gone through.

Well, it's not anything sensational, I don't know what you're expecting. But in my opinion it's interesting and instructive enough.

Because it's so common.

Consequently it interests a person.

He's thirty-six, she's thirty.

It started when she was on vacation at her grand-mother's in Červenky and nearly drowned. That was in 1940. She was fourteen. And he was twenty.

Of course, I didn't know them at the time. I know about this secondhand, partly from what Polly herself told me, partly from Lizette.

Lizette's apartment plays a role in this.

As does Lizette herself.

In 1940 Lizette was already a woman. With heels, breasts, lipstick, etc. She started early, with immediate success. They swarmed around her like the mindless bugs who fall for those ball-shaped, meat-eating plants in South America.

They marched right up, in double time.

And in line with all the others was Pollyanna. She loved her, as sometimes happens, so passionately that she wept away June nights. Letters, caresses, kisses, etc.—if she hadn't been fourteen years old, it would have fallen under the jurisdiction of the law against the third sex, which was still strictly enforced back then.

Lizette used her to run errands. Other than that, she didn't give a damn about her.

And while Pollyanna was carrying letters and notes and messages to Lizette's admirers and toadies, she naturally began to feel a little sorry that none of them were for her.

When she nearly drowned and Arnošt Karásek jumped into the Vltava in his Sunday pants, things came to a head.

The things that are always accompanied by mystery.

As in this case. Karásek fell for her, from his toes to the top of his ducktail *eman* haircut, which in those days was still called a *havel*. He fell for the fourteen-and-a-half-year-old, dark, bony teenager with eyes like a frightened Indian monkey.

The same cannot be said of Pollyanna. But because he committed himself to her completely and because Lizette had a hoard of men and she had no one, she started to go out with him.

Go out, that is. At that age and in that era, it was not yet a synonym for sleeping together.

Naturally, a boy from Červenky, whether consciously and calculatingly, or unconsciously and instinctively, had goals in mind.

He set out to take her by storm.

But Pollyanna held the field. Lizette was there to offer wise and malicious advice.

She had this theory on the subject:

1: Kisses are the first step toward sex.

2: One should always finish what one begins.

3: A woman should be a princess, which means that she should only have one man in her lifetime.

Unfortunately I have to say that Lizette adhered to these principles only more or less. That is, insofar as they suited her.

But what the master does perfectly and with seeming thoroughness, the disciple-martyrs only bungle.

Pollyanna was soon mired in contradictions. She started kissing, but then she didn't want to finish what she'd begun.

She did seem like a princess, a real-life princess of course, not a fairy-tale one.

Lizette did not take into account that princehood is in reality more or less a governmental function and the prince's connection with the princess's sexual life is more or less symbolic.

But that would be getting ahead of my story.

Consequently Arnošt stormed and Pollyanna parried.

Out of despair he got involved in underground activities.

Arnošt, you should know, has freckles and a short temper. When something doesn't work out for him, he immediately gets drunk and plunges into despair. At that time, despair was a first for him.

He left for the Reich, where he became a spy.

At least that's what he said.

In any case after the revolution they gave him medals.

And that's when Pollyanna succumbed.

It happened in the Andre Hotel, Arnošt was in an

Afrikakorps uniform with a Revo-Loot-ionary armband on his sleeve and he gave the maid a five-hundred-crown tip for the bloodstained sheet.

He was always big about these things.

But in this case things somehow didn't quite work out for him.

For this deflowering had strange consequences, as experiments like this sometimes have.

Arnošt went mad with passion.

Pollyanna lost all interest in him.

This is when the years of calvary began, a martyrdom that seems, when I glance out at the dance floor, to continue to this day.

It dragged out—or is dragging out—in periodic systoles and diastoles; see, Pollyanna alternately took him in and set him adrift.

As a rule, when she was attracted to someone with whom she hoped to experience Love, etc., it was Lent for Arnošt, and when she recognized she wasn't experiencing Love, he was allowed to come back again.

For there are two things here: Love, which has the habit of not existing, and Habit, which exists for goddamn sure.

Some people, mind you, have the good fortune, blessedness, ability, grace, lunacy, or whatever it is to experience Love. Usually they're nebbishes.

So maybe they just talk themselves into it.

By Love I mean Love that lasts a lifetime.

But by and large it always blows over in the long run. Later, sooner, too soon.

The first time she rejected Arnošt, he staged a scene worthy of the National Theater, so that Polly got scared and made the bed.

I met her just when the second period of rejection was reaching its climax.

At that time I had the opportunity—as did Polly-anna—to observe the auspicious blooming of Lizette's Love for Robert, while I was left high and dry with respect to my affections for that princess. Observing this happy relationship also frayed Pollyanna's nerves not a little. Karásek went off on a slimming cure, and Polly started to search for a Love of her own with all her might.

Let me tell you, these kinds of attempts are hopeless. If you start to search, you've got it all wrong.

Because of course you can't search for these kinds of things.

Either they come or they don't.

The tragedy is, they usually don't.

That's the law of nature.

The messy part here was the fact that Pollyanna had her eye on me. As soon as she laid out the case with her big black eyes like a frightened monkey in the jungle, I said: Hey.

Hey, I said later.

Hey, Lizette said afterward. If you want to roll in the hay with Pollyanna, don't come crawling around my place.

Since a person is selfish where what he thinks is most important is concerned, within a single revolution of this earth on its axis, I didn't give a damn about Pollyanna.

I was sitting in Lizette's room the next day and I was talking to her like the Song of Songs, in order to appease her, when Pollyanna darted in, her eyes like an orangutan that had been frightened to death, and she handed us a letter.

She wasn't angry at me.

She was always really great that way.

In the letter Arnošt Karásek declared that he would wait until Friday for an answer in the affirmative. If he did not receive this answer by Friday evening at eight o'clock, he would lode his gun.

That's how he spelled it.

He wasn't entirely literate.

Pollyanna: What do I do now?

Look, didn't Arno say he was going to sell his Bugatti? Lizette asked.

That's what he said, Pollyanna replied.

Let's go, Lizette ordered.

Along the way she explained the plan.

I was supposed to pass myself off as a certain engineer Cincibus or something, interested in buying the Bugatti, who would go to Červenky to look at it on Saturday.

On Saturday, get it? When the question of whether

Karásek lived till Saturday supposedly depended on Pollyanna.

I was for it; we called long-distance from the post office and in five minutes Arno was on the line. When I mentioned the Bugatti, it sparked his interest. He didn't talk like a suicide at all. He temptingly described the acceleration, how it handled, how much it guzzled per hundred kilometers. He told me in detail how to get to Červenky. Not until the end of the interview did something occur to him, maybe, because he pricked up his ears and wanted to know who had told me about this bargain.

I pretended there was something wrong with the phone line and cleared out of the phone booth.

I assured Pollyanna nothing would happen. Lizette made some cruel remarks and Polly calmed down.

And then Saturday morning a telegram arrived for Polly: Please come, I'm in the hospital. And—

—I have to say, he *was* in the hospital. When he didn't get an answer to his ultimatum, he shot himself. He said he aimed for his heart, but his hands were shaking so badly from excitement and rage that he shot into muscle above the elbow.

Simply put, he hadn't hit his heart, but technically he had attempted suicide.

This was Polly's predicament.

What could she do: I wasn't working out for her as Love, so she went back to him.

Later she found out that he sold the Bugatti while he was still in the hospital.

At that time Arnošt was working as the director of all the coal-mining work teams in Ostrava district and he earned fifteen thousand a month. But he was no miser. It would be more accurate to say he had those fifteen thousand on the first of the month. In the evening he would get on the plane to Prague and the next day usually he didn't have them anymore. We all got hangovers from it. Me, Lizette, Robert, Zetka, the boys in the band, the brothers Mengele, everyone. And Polly the worst, of course.

Because she, poor thing, paid for his payday with her body.

And it dragged on like this for maybe another year. God knows if it had become habit, or if there was still compassion, or even in the end something like feeling.

Maybe the lack of any better opportunities.

This is at the bottom of almost all so-called great loves, and all of us, down to the last man and woman, make nothing but compromises.

From cradle to grave, as they say. It's not worth shit.

Excuse me.

Excuse me, ladies.

She went out with him in the figurative sense of the words and often we threw great parties. Maybe at the Mengele brothers' place, Theodore and Killian, madmen who avoided work and lived off the sale of pornographic photographs they manufactured themselves and even posed for, together with Killian's girl Vrát'a.

But what do you know, ladies. What do you know about the weight things have, the unbearable weight.

Not a damn.

But let me finish my story.

After a period of patience, it happened to Polly again. She longed for her so-called own life, i.e., for love.

We're all a little meshuggah now and then. From time to time everyone commits some sort of idiocy.

And she started up in two locations, with a Karel, who was a Communist, and with a Radoslav, who studied medicine.

Yeah, well—Polly was studying architecture.

At first Arno accomplished wonders. Drinking binges, scenes beneath her window, brawls, etc. Then he finally accepted it as the status quo and came to terms with his two colleagues.

They comprised a triumvirate.

What do you know about it.

But one day it blew up on Polly. Arnošt rushed into Lizette's place, his tie tangled around his back, his eyes like bloody moons, baring his teeth. Instinctively I sat down near the door, since I had Polly on my conscience, as you know, and with a temper like Arno's, you never know.

Disgusting, the pig, my God! Arno yelled, Italian-style. After a while it became clear that he'd subjected Polly to a physical inspection and discovered a disgusting thing. In the neck area she had seven blood-red contusions, technically known as hickeys.

Excuse my naturalism. I don't think another word for them exists.

Two had come from him. He remembered them. According to her own testimony, two were from Radoslav, one from Karel. Two and two plus one equals five.

But she had seven of them.

So who had she gotten the last two from?

She didn't know. She counted them wrong, that is, she had no idea how many she had, she got confused, and Arno had her cornered.

He insisted, begged, commanded, and finally whipped her with a belt. Then she confessed. A certain Jan Zábrana, 13 Birch Street, Prague, District XVI.

The impudence. On top of everything he lived on the same street where Arnošt's Prague apartment was.

And he was an architecture student.

A colleague, therefore.

Another time we were sitting at Lizette's, just her and me (Robert was out of town), right after an unsuccessful attempt at seduction on my part, a failure I was taking to heart.

I was feeling suicidal.

The doorbell rang.

Arnošt.

He staggered in, dressed in an Esterhazy suit and clutching a pigskin briefcase; the room immediately clouded up with alcohol fumes.

And he started roaring.

I.e., sobbing.

Lizette set about consoling him; suddenly Arno pulled himself together and again started roaring.

I.e., screaming.

That today he'll find out what's really going on, and if it turns out to be true, he'll shoot Polly and this guy, plus himself.

So what?

It appeared that he'd run into this architecture student and worked himself into a fury over his proprietary—or more precisely, shareholder's—rights to Pollyanna. And the guy took it calmly. Said it wasn't his doing, it was all Pollyanna. His role in the affair was entirely passive. All the activity issued from the girl's efforts. He would offer proof. That evening he was going to Pollyanna's for a tutoring session. It was a pretext devised for Pollyanna's parents, so he could come visit. He would leave the light on, and he wouldn't shut the window, which looked out on the garden. Arno could climb the pear tree in front of the window and decide for himself who was responsible.

At this point Arno stood up, shook off Lizette, pulled a filthy German automatic out of his briefcase, clicked the safety, and started waving it around, bawling.

Today he'd show them. All of them. All of them!

And he was looking at me.

I quickly forgot about suicide and slipped over to the couch, which was even closer to the door.

Then Arno pulled a Leica and a Swiss watch out of his briefcase. If anything should happen to him, these belonged to Lizette. For all she's done.

Then with a touch of pathos, he stepped out the door.

Lizette and I entertained ourselves with speculations about how it would turn out. We divvied up the things.

Lizette would keep the Leica, I'd get the Swiss watch. Outside it started to rain. For a while the heavens were absolutely prodigal with water.

The hours shuffled slowly by, until they stumbled up against two in the morning. Outside the window, the storm howled and howled.

At 2:05, Arno returned. No more Leica for Lizette.

No more Swiss watch for me.

Arno looked as if he were wearing a mud suit on top of his Esterhazy one. One of his cheeks was larger than usual, and in exchange, one of his eyes was smaller.

Yes. He'd climbed the pear tree and looked. He had a direct view of the divan. The guy came, stretched out, put his hands behind his head. Polly hopped on top, kissed him, caressed him, in short, behaved altogether immorally.

Arno shook with anger, and as he shook, so did the

branch beneath him. He fell to the ground with a loud crash, and the guy poked his head out the well-lit window.

Well? Did you see? Am I right or what?

Arno pounced on him and dragged him out of the window down into the garden.

They exchanged a few blows, then Polly ran up and Arno gave her one across the face.

The architect burst out laughing.

He got one across the face from Pollyanna and he left.

Yeah, but otherwise everything was fine, Arnošt and Pollyanna said a few words.

Then they started up with each other again.

In a gold locket around his neck, Arnošt carried a curl that didn't come from Pollyanna's black head of hair, and he photographed the girl in her birthday suit with his Leica. He showed us the photos; Lizette borrowed them from him and passed them around to others.

Then Pollyanna received a letter. Concise. Polly, for God's sake, come!

Yours, A., c/o Ostrava County Prison.

He wasn't even able to write out his name.

Nonetheless Polly went, and came straight back. Arno was in the slammer for the rape of a minor. For the girl, the consequences were serious nervous shock and moderate bodily harm; for him the consequence was the loss of a tooth, which a cop knocked out for him when they deprived him of his freedom, which seemed too high a price to pay without putting up a fight.

They took the girl off to the asylum.

All this while under the influence.

With a forgetfulness usual in a woman, Pollyanna declared this meant the end between them. Arno could swear oaths regarding the strength of his love till Gabriel blew his trumpet, but she wasn't going to let herself be two-timed by him.

Karel, Radoslav, that architect, they didn't count. Me—I absolutely didn't count.

She got it from Lizette.

Once a guy starts going with another girl, man overboard! That was her slogan.

I happened to suit Pollyanna as well.

And that's how she left it with Arno.

But that's not how no prior record and valuable service to society, etc., left it. Within a fortnight he was out with a suspended sentence. Immediately he got drunk. He flew to Prague and staged a scene, but Polly didn't give in.

In despair he took up with a woman named Božena, an editor's wife. And bang, serious love. Arno was thrilled. Božena too, of course.

She left her husband and children at once, and set up house with her lover. She was a strong little lady and she talked as though none of it had anything to do with her. Arno dragged her over to Lizette's and when she explained how she had liquidated her marriage, it was like she was reporting on foreign affairs. At first her husband was angry, but since she remained calm, he calmed down too. Then he asked her, Boža, before you go, lie down on the couch again, undress a little, once more before you leave for good . . . You could hear the three dots when she told the story. And she lay down, after all that one thing had always clicked between them, she took off her dress and splashed on a little perfume. Her husband came back from the kitchen, he was carrying something behind his back, and when he got up close to her, he pulled it out and it was a whip and he thrashed her naked backside.

That's what she told us.

All the while, she was eating Lizette's little open-faced sandwiches one after the other.

They divided up their possessions. She discovered that he had cut delicate incisions in both her skis with a hacksaw, so she would fall flat on her face when she went skiing that winter.

Arno was sitting beside her. From time to time he would stroke Božena's spherical attractions, somewhat lost in thought.

When she moved her wardrobe into Arno's efficiency at 16 Birch Street, they demolished the banisters.

I tried to picture Arno's studio, Božena's wardrobe, and Božena, all three together, and it didn't fit.

It was too much.

Arno got a little buzz on.

By the following Saturday he had caught gonorrhea in Ostrava and Saturday night he infected Božena.

But Bernard supplied them with penicillin, so they didn't get registered at the VD office. Yeah, Christ, Bernard the kleptomaniac, the one who got together with Iwain to part Geraldine from those two thousand crowns. Same guy. They employed him at the penicillin factory. And today—he's a student. The factory okayed him to go off and study biochemistry.

A doctor helped them out with penicillin for a largish smallish bribe.

Of course the serious love affair cracked up over this.

Or whatever it was.

Božena flew off to visit her aunt in Bratislava. By chance the editor was loitering there as well. They rode back together in the same sleeping car. They sent movers to pick up the wardrobe.

Arno got the bill for the movers.

He paid it.

He was big about it.

And Polly took him back out of the goodness of her heart.

So, ladies, do you get it yet?

More of Polly's loves ensued. I don't know which came first, Rais the psychiatrist or Fikola the army welterweight champion.

Then Arno married Ellinka and quickly divorced her.

Then Polly married a dentist named Sudrab and cheated on him for a year with Arno.

Then he divorced her.

Then—I don't know any more. It's a story that's always the same and probably will be. Arno came back to her bed like malaria, and maybe it is some kind of chronic disease. Maybe black-haired Pollyanna suffers from European malaria like everyone else who tries and searches and would like to give herself, but doesn't have anyone to give herself to.

Like everyone who's doomed that way. Who would have been better off if as spermatozoids they had thought twice before battling their way through the egg cell's rind.

But given the life span these spermatozoids have. Unpleasant. Senseless.

In the end they break into the cells, and this is what you get.

Pollyanna, for example.

And so they march to the rhythm of the boogie-woogie, I philosophically play out for them my eight eighth notes per measure, and Marcela Růžičková sings a running commentary with the words of a classic blues song, which she's adapted to the female gender:

I can't use no man
If he can't help me lose the blues . . .

Maybe it'll go on like this for another twenty or thirty years.

There's nothing that would save them from it.

There's no saving some people.

Some people are put here only to join society's efforts and through their labor to build the world that other people live in.

But they live.

Not like Polly and the rest of them here.

Dialogus De Veritate

Pilate saith unto him: What is truth?

ST. JOHN, 19:38

That fellow reminded me of someone the moment he arrived. He came in about nine, and sat down at a table right under the stage. He looked exactly like somebody I knew, but who?

He ordered a carafe of wine and stared at me. After a while it got on my nerves. One glass after another, and the guy stares and sips and gapes. Damn!

Sure, there are hepcats who gawk. They gawk at your fingers, at your sax, at your face. But you can tell they're music fans. This guy was staring at me, not at the way I made music.

During break, as I got up to go to the toilet, I saw the guy getting up, too. And sure enough, as soon as I found myself among the tiles and started to relieve myself, he was right beside me, legs spread wide, staring up at me!

That really made me mad.

Look here, mister, I started, but he just lowered his eyelids and said: Hi, Smiřický.

And then I recognized him.

Dunca Brom.

I almost pissed on my pants, I was so startled.

Pardon me, ladies. Pardon me.

Dunca savored my embarrassment, and then said:

Sure, it's me, personally, minus mustache. And my hair got darker.

I swear to God. Dunca used to be blond, and now he was as black as an eclipsed sun.

And the Gable mustache was gone.

I looked around. The sign on one of the toilet doors read: OCCUPIED. I put my finger on my lips, and Dunca smirked.

Great. Is that something new around here? A kind of secret Masonic sign?

That's right, I said. Let's go. We sat down at his table. I glanced at the stage. Nobody was there yet, and people were still chatting in the hall. I turned to Dunca.

This really is a surprise . . .

I need a place to stay, he said matter-of-factly.

That put me in a painful situation. I would have enjoyed shooting the bull with him, that wasn't it—the problem was simply . . . Well, I've always been a champion of caution, staying out of trouble, neutrality. That was my kind of wisdom. And it always paid off for me. And now, suddenly . . .

Natch, I said. Or rather, my mouth said it. Naturally. After all, I couldn't bear to lose face. Not after that unquestioning confidence he had shown me.

Where do you live? Still on Rajský Hill?

Right. Everything's still the same.

Dunca raised his eyebrows. Sure, it was him. That slightly too handsome, movie-star kisser under that new shock of black hair.

Everything?

Natch, I said. That's obvious, isn't it?

Great, he answered. I see that I knocked on the right door.

Unfortunately, I thought to myself. But aloud, I said: So what's been happening? Tell me.

Let's wait till we get home, OK? Hey, look at that pretty chick over there, he said, and winked at a sultry brunette a la Dolores del Rio. But I think her name was Havašíková, or something like that.

The brunette responded with a vague smile.

Knockout knockers, said Dunca.

Sure, it was him all right.

Zetka and Davida climbed up on the stage.

I've got to go now, I said. Shall I wait for you afterward?

Don't worry, he said, and got up. I got up on stage and we started with *Bigwig in the Wigwam.* I watched him and saw him spinning Del Rio–Havašíková around her own axis on the dance floor.

I didn't feel good about the whole thing. I know from experience—other people's, not my own—that once you stick your foot in the water, you'll end up dripping wet sooner or later.

But there are certain situations . . . All I had to do was to go to the phone, dial—and I'd be in the clear. In fact, I'd greatly improve my political rating.

Needless to say, nothing like that entered my mind. I am a coward, a parasite, a hipster, I am lazy and often use vulgar expressions in mixed company. I have plenty of other faults as well.

But I am not a scoundrel.

And so at midnight, after the last number, I wiped the sax dry, picked up my windbreaker and headed for Dejvice. A trolleybus took me up Rajský Hill. Dunca was nowhere to be seen. Only after I unlocked the garden gate did he emerge out of the shadows. That's the first sight I had of him since watching him twirl Havašíková on the dance floor.

Man, he had really learned how to keep a low profile.

I closed the gate, we quickly walked up the path to the house and upstairs to my room. As soon as I turned on the light Dunca plunged into an armchair.

Don't worry, he said as if he read my mind. My buddy with whom I was supposed to stay tonight is arriving tomorrow. I'll be gone by morning.

No problem, I said. I was as full of sudden happiness as an amnestied prisoner.

In my joy, I just couldn't do enough for him. Would you like some coffee? Or a drink?

What have you got? he asked mistrustfully. I opened the liquor cabinet, where I had half a bottle of Key Island rum and some Pont Neuf brandy from Hungary. Dunca took one look, and said: Just give me some coffee.

While I was making coffee we kept silent. I brought two cups to the table and sat down facing Dunca.

Here we are, he said.

Man, I said, how in hell did you get involved in that stuff?

He shrugged: A man should change his occupation once in a while, otherwise he grows stale. I discovered I had an unsuspected talent.

It would seem that way, I said.

He threw me a dirty look.

Why don't you try it too, chum?

No way. That's not my cup of tea.

You know English, he said, ignoring my last remark. You've got a nose for opportunities. He glanced around. I'd guess that this cozy little flat is the fruit of considerable diplomatic talent. In fact, given the present circumstances, one might say an unhindered talent.

Sure, but . . .

Here you're just shit, and you'll stay shit. As long as those jerks stay in power, you'll stay shit. You know that, don't you?

Sure, but . . .

And you don't want to give up jazz, he said.

Look here, Dunca, I said. Let's get things clear. I'm shit, and I'll stay shit as long as those jerks are around. But it's better to be shit than a number in a striped shirt, don't you agree?

Good Lord. You talk like Dolores Ibarruri La Passionaria, only ass-backwards.

And so I prefer sitting here on Rajský Hill than some-where else. Like a refugee camp in Krautland.

He seemed to turn sad. But he was probably just play-acting.

Et tu, mi fili, he said mournfully. You starting to believe those jerks?

Nonsense, I answered. But quite a few decided to come back, didn't they.

Listen to me, Dunca said. You'd have no need or de-sire to come back. Fools, cowards and total zeroes come back. But not anybody with an ounce of brains in his skull. Except the way I came back.

OK, I said.

Seriously. We'll make a deal and I'll get you out.

No thanks.

There'll be absolutely no risk as far as you're con-cerned, Dunca said. I'm doing it strictly out of friendship. I'll just take care of a little business here and then you'll get a free ride. I have a guaranteed leak, don't you worry.

I see, I said, and started to perspire.

Believe me, a piece of cake. No crawling on our bel-lies, no cutting of barbed wire. A big shot in the border guards is in with us. It'll be like a stroll along the Moldau.

Listen, Dunca. I believe everything you say and I'm grateful to you for thinking of me, but no. Thanks a lot, re-ally, but no.

He probed deep in my eyes.

So you really don't want to?

No.

You're scared, aren't you!

No, I answered, although I was. But actually it wasn't so much a matter of fear. At least, it wasn't the fear of frontier guards or anything like that. It was something else.

You're lying, Dunca said. You're a shitass, like you always were.

Have it your way, I said. If that's what you think . . .

I have friends in Radio Free Europe. You're a born storyteller. You could sell them stuff for good money. You know lots of stories, you were always good at making up stories. And there's your sax . . .

No, Dunca, forgive me, but it's no deal.

But why, for heaven's sake? Do you ever think about what goes on around you?

This might surprise you, but I think about it all the time. Maybe you think it's crazy, Dunca, but I'm a socialist.

Listen, man, I'll believe everything else, but not that.

You don't have to.

But even if you were, which I don't believe for a minute—what does that have to do with this country? Is this your idea of socialism?

Something along those lines, I said.

Dunca stared at me, wide-eyed. Along what lines? We had a similar bunch here not long ago, if you remember, along national socialist lines. They didn't care much for jazz, either.

Listen, I said. I may not be crazy about the Party or about the government. I'm only trying to be objective.

Just like the people's supreme tribunal, said Dunca.

First of all: if I came with you, I'd probably starve.

I told you I have friends in Radio FE.

Maybe you do, but I'd never work for them. I'm not a political animal. Politics demands that you get all worked up and bullshit about ideals. That's not my style.

But you say you're a socialist, Dunca objected.

I know it sounds funny, but yes, something along those lines.

Along their lines? All those stupidities of theirs you see all around you, they don't bother you?

They bother me.

And what about all the rest of their swill?

Listen, I said. I know about the swill better than you do. I see jerks and idiots in high places who know as much about governing as a pig knows about pianos. And they play with people's lives like it was all a big game.

And yet you're something like a socialist, said Dunca.

Because this regime has little to do with socialism.

There I agree with you, Dunca said. Except maybe of the national kind.

Nobody is going hungry, I said.

You don't seem to be well-informed, said Dunca. Just

ask a retired fellow trying to manage on a two-hundred-crown pension. I guess that such people must atone for the good jobs they had before the war.

Even if that's true, you're talking about a small minority. The vast majority have plenty to eat. I sensed that I was just beating my gums, and felt like an awkward fool.

You're going to make me puke, said Dunca. You babble about hunger like a political instructor after a week's schooling. Have you ever gone hungry?

No. And neither has anybody else.

Christ Almighty, said Dunca. And it doesn't bother you that you've got to turn yourself into a whore? Think one way and talk another, suck up to people you'd rather kick in the ass? Keep turning around to see who's behind you, keep your finger on your lips like it was glued there?

I don't like these things any more than you do. But if you insist on talking about it . . . Sweat poured down my back. I'm bullshitting, I thought to myself, I've blown it. I said: It's all a matter of a scale of values. I believe—not because I like it, but because it's probably the truth—that the highest value, to put it crudely, is a full stomach. Because that's a law of nature. And also the certainty that I'll always have the possibility of making a living. And when I won't be able to work any longer, the state will take care of me.

You seem to think of socialism as a system for producing pensioners.

Something like that, I said.

And you believe that? Dunca said, gaping straight at me.

No. I don't know. I only believe: some day. I simply believe in decently dressed people, guys on motorcycles and girls in nylon blouses.

A new stage of Marxism, Dunca grumbled. Nylon socialism. The way it looks to me, your ideas of the West come out of *Progressive Perspectives*. Torn pants and starved, sunken faces.

Maybe not now, I said, and my shirt felt like it was pasted to my back. But once a depression hits . . .

Straight out of *Progressive Perspectives,* Dunca broke in. Listen: I bet they taught you that during the Depression, America had twelve million unemployed, while the USSR didn't have a single one.

Well, isn't it the truth? I said, and glanced at my feet to make sure sweat wasn't dripping out of my trouser legs.

It is, Dunca nodded. But what they didn't tell you is how many people they had stashed away in Siberian concentration camps.

Maybe you're right. I never thought of that. I shifted in my chair. My pants, too, were beginning to stick to my body.

So it's just about fifty-fifty, said Dunca. You can choose between northern lights and unemployment insurance.

I fell silent.

And all this nonsense they've got here, Dunca said.

Do you think it's necessary? Do you think there's no other way to introduce socialism?

I don't know, I said. They introduced it here.

Yeah. But seriously: do you really put the full stomach of some beer-guzzling lout higher than culture? Higher than that jazz of yours, higher than a life worthy of human beings?

I turned stubborn.

First you've got to have a full stomach before you can . . .

Dunca shook his head. *Progressive Perspectives.* All right, I give up.

I shrugged.

Dunca suddenly flared up: You really believe, he said, his voice quivering with excitement—that if these bastards ever succeed in gobbling up the world—you think that under their wise leadership the world will be worth a shit, you think life will be worth a damn?

I don't necessarily believe that, I said, beginning to feel feverish. I simply don't know. Probably—yes.

Can't you see, since you claim you know them so well, that all they'll ever accomplish is to eliminate hunger, maybe, and maybe they'll even play Beethoven, but you can bet they won't produce any new Beethovens. And if by some error of planning one were to appear, they'd make sure he wrote odes to the Party rather than odes to joy. Is this bunch of bastards going to save the world? At best they'll turn the world into a well-fed prison. But of course, for you a full stomach is the highest possible value.

For the time being, I guess it is. Of course, if things ever turn out the way you described, then it's a different matter.

If, according to you, a full stomach is the highest value of life, Dunca said, speaking very slowly, then be good enough to tell me: how is a human life different from that of a cow or a pig?

The conversation was really upsetting me. I was soaking down to my shoes. What the hell was the point of all this, what did I know about politics, anyway? I'd much rather have played my sax for him, but it was getting close to dawn.

For the present, there is probably very little difference.

That silenced Dunca.

We gabbed a bit more, but in the end Dunca got disgusted, lay down and fell asleep, and I went to the bathroom to hang things up to dry.

I admired his nerves. If I were in his situation, I wouldn't be able to sleep a wink.

In the morning, he said good-bye.

You change your mind about coming? he asked.

No, Dunca. Forgive me.

Well, OK then. Ahoy, and thanks!

Thanks, and lots of luck, I said.

Then he disappeared.

This was two months ago, and I haven't seen him or heard about him since. I kept reading *Progressive Perspectives,* but there was no mention of any arrest.

So that's the story. I play the sax, and continue living here. I don't want to get involved. Maybe it isn't just a matter of fear. I don't know. All I know is that I don't want to get involved.

Maybe you think I'm a jerk. But everything I told you, about getting nabbed, about Geraldine, Kambala, Lizette and all the rest, that's the God's own truth.

Then again, what do I know about the truth, or about the way things are going to turn out. Pilate, that's me.

As for myself . . .

But I've gabbed long enough.

And forgive me, ladies, for the vulgarities that crept in here and there. I'm really sorry about that. If I'm ever able to get this published, I'll drop all the dirty words and put in decent expressions. You'll pick them out yourselves.

You see how I respect and honor you.

So maybe I'm not such a bad fellow after all.

With your permission, I take my leave.

Sweet dreams.

Good night.

—Written 1954-1956 in Prague

About the Author

Josef Škvorecký was born in Bohemia and emigrated to Canada in 1968. He and his wife, the novelist Zdena Salivarová, run a Czech-language publishing house, Sixty-Eight Publishers, in Toronto. Škvorecký's novels include *The Cowards, Miss Silver's Past, The Bass Saxophone, The Engineer of Human Souls, Dvorak in Love, The Miracle Game, The Republic of Whores, The Bride of Texas,* and most recently *Headed for the Blues.* He has also written many short stories and film scripts, and is the winner of the 1980 Neustadt International Prize for Literature and the 1984 Governor General's Award in Canada.